SUGAR CREEK GANG
The BROWN BOX MYSTERY

Paul Hutchens

MOODY PRESS
CHICAGO

ISBN: 0-8024-7031-9

1 3 5 7 9 10 8 6 4 2

Printed in the United States of America

PREFACE

Hi—from a member of the Sugar Creek Gang!

It's just that I don't know which one I am. When I was good, I was Little Jim. When I did bad things—well, sometimes I was Bill Collins or even mischievous Poetry.

You see, I am the daughter of Paul Hutchens, and I spent many an hour listening to him read his manuscript as far as he had written it that particular day. I went along to the north woods of Minnesota, to Colorado, and to the various other places he would go to find something different for the Gang to do.

Now the years have passed—more than fifty, actually. My father is in heaven, but the Gang goes on. All thirty-six books are still in print and now are being updated for today's readers with input from my five children, who also span the decades from the '50s to the '70s.

The real Sugar Creek is in Indiana, and my father and his six brothers were the original Gang. But the idea of the books and their ministry were and are the Lord's. It is He who keeps the Gang going.

PAULINE HUTCHENS WILSON

1

It might have been a long, hot, boring summer for the three members of the Sugar Creek Gang that were left—and there were *only* three of us left, Poetry, Dragonfly, and me—if all of a sudden one of the most interesting, exciting, and dangerous experiences hadn't exploded like a Fourth of July firecracker right in front of our eyes.

That stormy, mysterious, dangerous, and upside-down experience came to life the first week after Big Jim, Circus, and Little Jim left Sugar Creek territory to be gone for two whole weeks. Big Jim and Circus were to work on Big Jim's uncle's farm in Tippecanoe County, and Little Jim would visit a cousin in Wisconsin.

The mystery started the week the new Bay Tree Inn Motor Court was finished and had what is called "open house." Our family as well as maybe everybody else's family in the neighborhood went to see it. Well, not *all* our family went—just Mom and Dad and me—because Charlotte Ann, my chubby little cute-nosed sister, had been left to be baby-sat at Dragonfly's house.

There wasn't anything Charlotte Ann would rather do, anyway, than be baby-sat by Dragonfly's mother, who nearly always gave her a new toy. She also let her play house with a set of pink plastic dishes and do almost anything in the world she wanted to do that wasn't dangerous.

I never will forget what my mother said to my father when the three of us were alone in Unit 17 at the Bay Tree Inn. That neat little cottage had been named Cliff Cottage and had been built by the management for people who wanted to stay quite a ways away from the sounds and sights of tourists in the sixteen other units. It sort of hung on the rim of a sandstone cliff overlooking a deep ravine, the same ravine, in fact, through which flows the small stream the gang calls "the branch."

Except for Sugar Creek itself, we liked the branch better than any other stream in the county. You could follow its sometimes lazy, sometimes nervous and excited and noisy, way from its source all the way through Harm Groenwold's woods and pasture, then into and through Thompsons' woods to where it finally empties at the mouth of the branch, where most of the time the gang keeps its boat tied.

Poetry, who is always reading interesting things and thinking up different ideas to make people laugh, has said maybe a hundred times, "The branch can lie in bed all day and run all over the county at the same time."

And Dragonfly, who also has a keen mind, nearly always answers him with: "It doesn't just *lie* in bed, it *runs* in bed—and not just all day but all night and, like a certain friend of mine, it's also all wet."

Anyway, standing near the picture window of Cliff Cottage's air-conditioned living room, Mom looked out and across the footbridge that spanned the ravine and said, "You couldn't find anything more picturesque at Turkey Run State Park, or at The Shades, or even in Brown County."

Brown County was the beautiful hill country Mom had been born and brought up in and where she had been a schoolteacher and a secretary before Dad had found her and married her to make her a farmer's wife.

Dad was standing beside Mom with his left arm halfway around her. Looking out that same window, he remarked, "If anybody taking a walk out there on the overhanging porch, or across the footbridge, should accidentally lose his balance and topple over, he would land like a ton of bricks on the rocks below and break a lot of bones. It's a good thing they have that iron railing all the way across."

Mom's answer was: "Not a ton but only one hundred forty-seven pounds. And not of bricks but of a hot, tired, and worn-out housewife who would like to spend a few days' vacation here away from washing, ironing, cooking, looking after the chickens, answering the telephone, canning cherries, raspberries, corn, and beans, and keeping her patience with two noisy children."

I was standing behind my parents near the fireplace at the time. I had just come in to ask an important question that Poetry Thompson, my almost best friend, who was just outside the door, wanted me to ask. It was a *very* important question—one of the most important questions I might ever ask.

Hearing Mom say she needed a vacation from her two noisy children, I accidentally on purpose cleared my throat.

She turned a startled face in my direction, grinned, and remarked, "My first and worst son excepted, of course."

Being called their "first and worst" son by my parents was their way of saying I was the only son they had and that they liked me. So I grinned back at my first and worst mother and answered, "Your first and *best* son agrees with you. You do deserve a vacation, and I know a way I can help raise money to help your first and worst *husband* pay for it."

That seemed a good way to get to do what my mind was all excited about getting permission to do—in fact, what Poetry and I already had our minds made up to do. And all that was needed was to get our parents to agree to it.

When for a minute neither my mother nor my father answered me, I managed to say, "Of course, if you wouldn't *want* the money, I could save it for a very badly needed two-week vacation for myself, just as soon as Big Jim and Circus and Little Jim get back. In fact, you could take *your* vacation right here in Cliff Cottage while the gang is having a north woods camping trip, which we haven't had for quite a few summers—if I can remember that far back."

Dad answered my suggestion by reminding me that six boys he knew had had a *winter* vacation not so long ago. "You *do* remember when the gang flew to Palm Tree Island, don't you?"

For a few seconds I let myself remember the gang's wonderful trip to the West Indies. First, our plane had sailed high out over small islands called the Florida Keys. As we'd looked down at them, Poetry had said that they looked like the "disjointed vertebrae of the backbone of the skeleton of a giant, hundred-mile-long dinosaur."

Then, after only a hundred or more or less minutes in the plane, we had landed at the Palacia airport. Palacia was the capital of Palm Tree Island. There we were welcomed by a missionary friend of Old Man Paddler's and by hundreds of excited, friendly, Spanish-speaking people.

It was while we were on that vacation on Palm Tree Island that we found Seneth Paddler's long-lost twin brother, Kenneth.

For another few seconds, while I was still standing by the fireplace in the Cliff Cottage living room, my mind's eye saw Kenneth Paddler, long-bearded and looking exactly like his brother, riding down one of Palacia's cobblestone streets in a small cart. He was driving a billy goat, an honest-to-goodness billy goat.

My father's voice broke into my memories of the gang's West Indies vacation as he leveled his gray green eyes at me. "Was there something special you wanted to say about how you could earn a little extra money this summer to help make it possible for your hardworking father, who *never* gets a vacation, to go *with* your mother when she goes on *her* vacation?"

What on earth! I thought. Imagine a boy's *father* needing a vacation. "You mean you get tired of planting and plowing corn, feeding hogs, making speeches at Farm Bureau meetings, milking cows, and building fences? Or are you just tired of having to put up with a son you wouldn't *have* to put up with if you would send him off to camp somewhere—maybe in the north woods?"

"Good try." Dad grinned and added, "But I believe you were talking about your first and worst *parents'* vacation."

I came out then with what was on my mind, beginning with, "Do you like fried frogs legs?"

Mom whirled around from the picturesque view across the gully, looked at me with an exclamation point in her brown eyes, and asked, "What kind of question is that?"

Maybe I should have told you—for about a week at our house we had been having a lot of family fun pretending we were actors in a play, having listened to what is called a "mock trial" the week before at the Sugar Creek Literary Society.

Sometimes I was a lawyer and Mom was the jury. My smallish sister, Charlotte Ann, was being tried for such crimes as spilling her milk, pulling up a petunia instead of a weed, or leaving the screen door open and letting our old black-and-white cat in. Things like that. Nearly always my father was the judge, and he would do what is called "pronounce sentence."

So when my brown-eyed mother asked me there in the Cliff Cottage, "What kind of question is that?" I could feel my father's gray green eyes boring into me from under his reddish brown brows, asking the same question.

"If it please the court," I began, "I am not the criminal in this case. I am the defense attorney, and my client is an honest boy."

For a minute I actually felt I *was* a lawyer, as Poetry's father had been in the mock trial. I swaggered over to the picture window that overlooked the limestone cliff on the other side and said, "See that little thread of water away down there at the bottom of the gully? That friendly little stream laughs and dances like an innocent barefoot boy through Harm Groenwold's woods and on through his pasture, through Thompsons' woods, and finally empties into Sugar Creek at the place known as the mouth of the branch, sacrificing its happy, carefree life to the larger, well-known creek shown on the map as Sugar Creek. Now, Your Honor, it so happens that the boys of the Sugar Creek Gang keep their boat tied there—"

In my mind I was back at the mock trial. It felt good being able to think on my feet, better than it does sometimes when I am alone in the woods yelling out Lincoln's Gettysburg Address to the trees and birds and frogs. I swung around then to my parents, who in my mind had just become the jury, and went on.

"Last night, while Leslie Thompson and his friend, William Jasper Collins, son of the famous Farm Bureau speaker, Theodore Collins, were sitting in their boat fishing for catfish, they noticed that over on the island among the willows and pickerel weeds maybe a hundred bullfrogs were having a Farm Bureau meeting, bellowing and croaking and having the time of their lives.

"In the frogs' meeting, one big shaggy-browed father frog stood up and bellowed: 'Fellow members of this convention, the Bay Tree Inn Dining Room has listed on its menu at a charge of ten dollars per dinner, chicken-fried Sugar Creek frogs legs. I have just learned that two of the boys of the Sugar Creek Gang have read that menu and have decided to go into business as the Sugar Creek Frogs Legs Supply Company. The Bay Tree Inn management has offered them fifty cents for every pair of frogs legs they bring in—a paltry sum, for legs as large as ours.'"

I stopped in my speech—it was a little hard to be my father and a bullfrog at the same time. But it did feel good to have my parents listening without interrupting, so I quickly went on, hurrying a little to get in what was on the frog speaker's mind. "'One of the boys of the gang, the first and worst son of Theodore Collins, wants to earn enough money to pay for his parents' vacation, and it is up to the citizens of Frogs Legs Island to stop him. If the boys.*do* organize their company, they'll row their boat over here every night, shine their flashlights all around, blinding us, and fill their gunnysacks with us, and we'll all be chicken fried.'

"The big, handsome bullfrog father finished his speech, let out a scared croak, and sank like a submarine into the shallow water. The maybe one hundred other frogs at the convention went *ker-plunk* under at the same time, because maybe Leslie Thompson or William Jasper Collins had thrown a rock over toward the island and scared them all half to death."

Right away I turned myself into the judge. I swung back from the picture window I had been looking out of and asked, "Lady and gentleman of the jury, have you reached a verdict?"

The gentleman of the jury, who was also the foreman, answered, "We have, Your Honor. We find the defendant guilty!"

Quicker than a frog's croak, my father became the judge, sentencing me with lowered eyebrows and stern words. "You, first and worst son, are hereby sentenced to membership on the governing board of the Sugar Creek Frogs Legs Supply Company. When do you begin operations?"

From behind me, a boy's voice broke in to say, "Tonight, sir." It was the friendly, ducklike voice of Leslie Poetry Thompson, who had come in while the frog was making his speech and who maybe had been listening to the whole thing.

Mom broke up the meeting then, saying,

"We'd better hurry on home. The mail will be there in—" she interrupted herself to look at her wristwatch, then finished her sentence "—in another thirty minutes."

"What's the rush?" the judge and gentleman of the jury asked. "I thought maybe you'd like to run on into town and shop around for that vacation lounging robe you've been looking in the catalogs for."

The lady of the jury gave the gentleman of the jury a smallish frown and said, "Oh, you!"

Then Mom added, "I'm sorry, but I won't be able to take any vacation this year. Not while my boss is on his own vacation."

"Your *boss*? Is that what I am to you?" Dad asked.

It seemed a good time for Poetry and me to go outside and discuss plans for our first trip to Frogs Legs Island that very night.

I knew what Mom meant about her "boss" being on vacation. Old Man Paddler had finished the last chapter of the book he had been writing, and my mother was typing it for him. The old man wasn't on a vacation exactly. He was in California visiting his nephew, who was on *his* vacation and wanted his uncle to come out and go fishing with him in the Pacific Ocean for codfish off the coast of Santa Cruz and for mackerel off the barge near Santa Ana.

Mom had been working every day during her spare time to get the book finished before the old man would get back. He had been gone for more than a week.

Being secretary for Old Man Paddler meant also that she had to look after his mail, which our mail carrier, Joe Sanders, left in Theodore Collins's box every day instead of in the old man's box up in the hills.

Nearly every day there had been a letter, and sometimes quite a few, from people who had read the old man's first book, *The Possible Man in the Impossible Boy,* and wanted him to explain something or other. And sometimes there would be a letter from somebody with a heavy heart who wanted him to pray for him or her.

Nearly every day, also, there would be a letter from missionaries, thanking him for praying for them and for helping pay their missionary expenses.

Being a private secretary, Mom was supposed to open all the mail to see if there was anything important enough to have to be forwarded to California.

One thing, especially, Mom was supposed to watch for—any news from Palm Tree Island about Kenneth Paddler. Soon after the Sugar Creek Gang found him, he had disappeared again, and the missionaries didn't know where he was. He had written one letter to his brother, Seneth, saying he hoped to come back to Sugar Creek as soon as he felt able to. But then, just as many years before when he had had amnesia, he'd just disappeared.

Anyway, while Mom and Dad were still talking inside the Cliff Cottage living room, Poetry and I took a walk across the narrow footbridge toward the other side of the ravine. We stopped about halfway across to look down at the very happy little branch, threading its way around among the rocks.

"Your big bullfrog father was right," Poetry remarked, leaning over the railing and focusing his eyes on the rocks the saucy little stream was tumbling around and over and through. "Anybody falling over the edge would *really* get hurt and—"

He stopped himself, exclaiming, "Listen!"

I didn't have to listen to hear what I was hearing, which was the sound of a motor way back in the woods somewhere. It sounded a little like an electric saw cutting down a tree or cutting a tree into fireplace wood.

We looked out into the dense woods and saw two motorcycles driving like crazy toward us along the path that bordered the branch. At the farther end of the bridge we were in the middle of, the riders slowed down, skidded to a stop, and looked across to where we were. It seemed that they weren't seeing us, though, but were looking past us to the large living room window of Cliff Cottage where Mom and Dad maybe still were.

They stopped only a few minutes, talking to each other, then both motors roared to life and took off back into the dense woods and up a steep hill. They dodged this way and that to miss trees and bushes and fallen logs, going in the direction of Harm Groenwold's apple orchard, which we knew was on the other side. Then they disappeared.

"Did you see what I saw?" Poetry asked.

What we had both seen was a name in large letters printed on the back of each of their red leather jackets. It was SONS OF LUCIFER.

"Maybe that is the name of their motorcycle club," Poetry guessed.

But those two motorcycles racing through the woods didn't seem very important right that minute while Poetry and I were planning our first big business venture.

How was I to know that that very night, while we would be on Frogs Legs Island, the Sons of Lucifer would explode us into a very dangerous adventure?

2

By the time my parents came out of Cliff Cottage to drive us home, Poetry and I had built up our hopes so high that we had saved almost a hundred dollars from the two hundred pairs of frogs legs we were going to harvest and sell to the manager of the Bay Tree Inn Dining Room. That would be fifty dollars apiece. We could have a lot of fun doing it, too, having had quite a lot of experience catching bullfrogs at night when all the gang was there. But, of course, this time there would be only the two of us.

So we planned, but we got our plans upset when we stopped at Dragonfly's house to pick up Charlotte Ann. The minute we pulled up to the mailbox under the silver maple tree at their place, Dragonfly came running like the wind toward us. He was carrying a copy of *The Sugar Creek Times*.

"Look!" he exclaimed. Then his face took on a mussed-up expression. He let out a sneeze and explained with a grin, "I might be allergic to the ink on this paper."

Right away his thoughts came back to where they had been, and he thrust the paper toward us, showing us a page he had marked with red pencil. It was an advertisement by the

Bay Tree Inn Dining Room and—of all things! —it included the *menu* Poetry and I had already seen, which had given us the idea of making a hundred dollars selling frogs legs that summer.

I hadn't seen Dragonfly so excited in a long time. "L–l–last night when we came home from visiting Uncle Quentin at Colfax, we stopped on the bridge so Mother could watch the lightning bugs above the island. Th–th–th–there was m–m–m–maybe a million bullfrogs whooping it up all up and down the creek. I'll bet we could sell all we could catch!"

Dragonfly's mother, with Charlotte Ann toddling along beside her, came out the Gilberts' front door then. My small sister was carrying a new blonde-haired doll in the crook of her arm. "Come on in a minute," Mrs. Gilbert called to my mother. "See what came in the mail this morning!"

And while the judge of the court and Old Man Paddler's secretary went into the Gilberts' house to see a new fur-collared coat Dragonfly's mother had ordered from a catalog, the only three members of the Sugar Creek Gang that were left organized the Thompson, Gilbert, and Collins Frogs Legs Supply Company.

Standing in the shade of the silver maple beside their mailbox, we made a three-cornered circle and agreed to divide our profits equally and to stand by each other "through thick and thin, for better or for worse, in sickness and in health, until death do us part."

It was Dragonfly's idea to use part of a wedding ceremony for what he called our "Pledge of Allegiance." Even though it wasn't anything new, it would have to do until we could think up something especially good for a frogs legs supply company.

Pretty soon the jury came back out, having decided Mrs. Gilbert's new fur-collared coat was not guilty of having anything wrong with it. Old Man Paddler's secretary, being a human being, came mincing across the yard toward Thompson, Gilbert, and Collins, wearing the new coat, as if she was a model in a women's style show.

And just then Dragonfly sneezed. He said to Poetry and me, "Mother might have to send it back. I might be allergic to the stimulated mink collar." And he sneezed again.

Poetry whispered to him, "The word is *simulated,* not *stimulated.*"

Dragonfly got a stubborn expression on his face and answered Poetry, "The word is *stimulated.* Dad says it's *stimulated* mink."

Seeing the Gilberts' mailbox, Mom decided we'd better hurry on home to get our own mail, so pretty soon we were spinning down the gravel road toward our place.

The minute we were in the driveway and had stopped, Mom was out of the car and taking a quick look in the box that said "Theodore Collins" on it.

It was empty.

"How come!" she complained to her husband. "The Gilberts already had *their* mail. It shouldn't take this long for Joe to get from there to here!"

"Don't you remember?" Dad reminded her. "They've changed the route a little. He drives down the lane between our south pasture and Groenwolds, delivers Harm's mail, circles back past the schoolhouse and Rogerses, then Thompsons, and finally stops here. We're one of the last stops on the route now."

Dad himself took a peek into the empty box, scratched his head, and remarked, "He should have been here by now, though."

We got special permission from the judge and his wife to make a fast trip down to the boat at the mouth of the branch. We wanted to make sure it was empty of water and that the oars were in their hiding place nearby, so that, as soon as it was dark enough, we could make our first trip to Frogs Legs Island, which the frog speechmaker had named the place.

Poetry and I swung onto our bikes and away we went *rickety-whirlety-sizzle* down the gravel road, stirring up a cloud of dust that sailed toward the woods in the direction of the leaning linden tree and the spring.

At the north road, we stopped in the shade of the big sugar tree, as we nearly always did to see if there were any new sale bills tacked on it, which there would be if anybody in the county was having a farm sale.

I was ready to take off, being in a hurry to get to the boat, when Poetry stopped me.

"Wait—I want to show you something!"

He stood his bike against the trunk of the big tree and waddled over to the rail fence, ordering me to follow him, which I did. A few feet from the fence, he slowed down and, shushing me, crept slowly toward what looked like a big new spiderweb. "Watch!" he ordered, and I watched impatiently as he stooped, picked up a firefly he found half buried in the grass, and threw it into the spider's web.

Quicker than the firefly could have given a fleeting flash, a big brown spider came driving out of his hiding place straight for the firefly. He seized it and—well, I turned away, always feeling sorry for anything that got caught in a spiderweb.

Maybe it was because Circus, one of the members of our gang, had almost lost his father once when he had been bitten by a black widow spider.

"Let's go," I said to Poetry.

He answered, "Yeah, let's! I could at least have fed the spider a centipede. I'm sorry!" Which proved my almost best friend *did* have a tender heart, and that is one reason he is my almost best friend.

In only a few minutes, our bikes reached the hill that leads down to the branch bridge, and there, not more than fifty feet from where the row of lilacs starts, was the red-white-and-blue mail truck and Joe Sanders sitting beside it in the shade of an elm tree.

"Flat tire," Joe said to us when we braked to

a stop. "I had one flat this morning when I was still in town. I left it for repair at the station, and now I've got another. Maybe on a day when I've planned a fishing trip right after dinner, I ought be *double* sure I have a spare with me."

"I used your phone," he said to Poetry, "and the station is sending a man out as soon as they can. But it's going to make delivery late for the rest of the people on this route."

"You have any mail for the Collinses and Old Man Paddler?" I asked.

Joe looked at his watch, then up the road to see if maybe his spare tire was coming. He said, "Not much for the Collinses but several letters and a package for Mr. Paddler. Oh, yes, there was a card for you—two, in fact."

He handed me two postcards, one from Seneth Paddler in California and addressed to William J. Collins, Secretary, The Sugar Creek Gang. The other was from Circus and Big Jim down in Tippecanoe County.

We read the card from Old Man Paddler first. It was written in his very careful, trembling longhand and said:

I am going to be away a little longer than I planned, so you boys can run up to the cabin Saturday to see how things are. The lawn will need mowing again. Yesterday I caught seventeen mackerel while fishing from the barge just off the coast from Santa Ana. Next winter, maybe, I'll fly you boys out for a few days just to see what saltwater fishing is like—and you can take in Disneyland while you're here.

My heart leaped with a glad feeling—even greater, it seemed, than when we had first found out we were going to get to vacation on Palm Tree Island.

"Good news?" Joe Sanders asked, but I was already reading the card from Circus and Big Jim, part of which was:

> We might not get to stay the full two weeks. There's a new law, we found out, that won't let a farmer hire a boy under sixteen to work for him, even if it is his own uncle. And if the boy *does* work, he can't get paid for it. So look for us home one of these days or nights.

The upper half of the card was in Big Jim's handwriting, and the lower half was from Circus, who wrote in green ink:

> We've been having a lot of fun with Big Jim's new tape recorder. Yesterday I sneaked up on a ruffed grouse while he was making his drumming noise. It sounded like a rubber ball bouncing a mile a minute on a tin roof. When we get back, we can tape our voices and all the different sounds in the swamp and along the creek.

Poetry asked Joe Sanders then, "Was there any mail for Leslie Thompson?"

"There was," Joe said. "I handed it to your mother when I made the call for the spare tire. It was your science magazine. It has an article on fireflies. Science has discovered what it is that makes them light up and—" Joe Sanders stopped, grinned, and explained, "I had a few minutes to spare, so I leafed through it—*after* I delivered it to your mother, of course."

Everybody on Route 4 liked Joe Sanders so much that we might not even care if he opened our *first-class* mail—which, of course, he wouldn't, because it would be against the law.

One of the letters for Old Man Paddler, as well as the package, was from an address on Palm Tree Island, I noticed. Would the letter—and maybe even the box—be from the old man's twin brother?

When I saw the foreign postmark, the idea hit me that if Joe would let me, I could take them home in a hurry just as soon as Poetry and I could make a flying run to the creek to see if the boat and the oars were there. That way Mom wouldn't have to wait for him to get his tire fixed.

It *seemed* like a good idea, but it wasn't.

"Sorry," Joe said, "but there's a law that won't let me give mail for somebody else to anyone under eighteen years of age. Are you eighteen or more?" he finished with a chuckle.

I wasn't and hadn't been for a long time.

"But I'm going right straight home," I objected, not liking to have my idea squelched.

Joe looked at Poetry and me and, in a serious voice, said, "These are days when too many people are keeping only the laws they happen to like. But laws, boys, are for obeying. Suppose, for instance, that I let you have your parents' mail and Mr. Paddler's. And suppose there was something of great importance in the letter and maybe in the box—something worth thousands of dollars. Just supposing, of course. And if for any reason you should lose it, you wouldn't like to visit me in jail, would you?"

Poetry cut into the conversation then and was smart enough to say, "We couldn't look through the bars at a nicer mail carrier."

Joe's face had a grin on it when he said, "I'd agree with you. Even my wife says so."

There was the sound now of a car coming from the direction of the Collins place, and it looked like a service truck. At the same time, from up the hill at Poetry's house, the dinner bell rang.

"That bell," Poetry announced, "means I have only thirty minutes to get ready to eat ham and eggs, apple pie, and maybe ice cream. Come on!" he ordered me. "Let's go see if the boat's OK for the grand opening of the Thompson, Gilbert, and Collins Company."

Leaving Joe and the mail truck with the maybe important mail in it, away we went, in a hurry to get to the creek where the boat was, so that Poetry wouldn't be too late to eat the lunch that would help him grow even bigger than he was.

The lilacs were in full bloom, my eyes and nose told me as I took off after my almost best friend for the mouth of the branch. Remembering how much Old Man Paddler's secretary liked lilacs, I decided to pick maybe five, and take them home when I went. I would stop at our toolshed, get an empty flower vase, fill it with fresh water from the iron pitcher pump, put the lilac stems in it, and carry them in to where Mom would be typing the old man's book—if she wasn't busy in the kitchen getting lunch. I would say, "Sweet fragrance to the sweetest member of the jury for—"

My sweet thoughts were interrupted by Poetry's yell from the creek. "Our boat's gone!"

Hearing him yell out like that with mad worry in his voice set my own worry on fire. I took off on the run to where he was. Breaking out into the open space by the maple sapling, I looked at the place where the boat was supposed to be. And Poetry was right—the floating stock of the Thompson, Gilbert, and Collins Frogs Legs Supply Company was gone!

3

The boat was not where we had left it and always kept it tied. And when we hurried to the secret hiding place where we kept the oars, they were gone, too!

There is only one thing you think at a time like that, and Poetry and I thought it and *said* it at the same time: *"Somebody has stolen our boat!"*

Having a detective-like mind, my almost best friend began to walk along the bank, looking for footprints or any other telltale signs that would give us a clue as to who the thieves might be.

I went this way, and he went that, and we both went both ways. But we didn't find anything suspicious—that is, not until Poetry, about a hundred feet from where we had started looking, let out a whistle, which brought me on the run to where he was.

He was standing in a little clearing bordered on one side by wild iris in bloom. In the center was a ring of ashes, a half-dozen empty tin cans, and, behind a log that might have been used for a bench, there was an almost empty box of facial tissues that still had several tissues in the bottom. Poetry held up a forefinger to his lips, as though maybe he thought somebody might be listening or spying on us.

Then he stooped, zipped out a tissue from the box, and with it picked up the very small butt of a cigarette.

Poetry lifted the brown stub to his nose, sniffed at it, and asked, "Ever smell tobacco like that?"

I smelled it, and I never had. It had a sickening odor, a little like the smell of a stepped-on overripe papaw or maybe the ripe-apple smell you get when you are close to a school of whirligig beetles, which cruise around in excited circles in shaded water near the shore, especially when the creek is quiet.

For a few seconds, while the smell of the cigarette stub was still in my nostrils, I was seeing with my mind's eye maybe a hundred small, black, oval water beetles circling round and round each other. And with my mind's ear I was hearing Dragonfly, the junior member of the Thompson, Gilbert, and Collins Frogs Legs Supply Company, sneeze and complain, "I'm allergic to ripe apples!" He did that every time we got too close to a milling stampede of whirligig beetles, which give off the most odor when they are scared or upset about something.

But it was only a fleeting flash of memory, because Poetry was already running toward the creek and calling over his shoulder, "I see it! Over there behind the willow!"

In a few half seconds I was where *he* was, and, sure enough, our boat was there, tied to the willow! And the oars were in it, not in their rowlocks but on the floor under the seats, so that if a wind would come up and rock the boat, swinging it around and back and forth, the oars wouldn't fall out and float downstream.

It felt good to know our boat was still there, but it *didn't* feel good to know somebody had taken it without asking any of us. And it was worrisome to think that whoever *had* borrowed it had moved it from the place where we kept it.

"Maybe we ought to keep it locked up and take the oars home whenever we are through with them," Poetry suggested. But quickly he changed his mind. "But we'd have to have six keys, and who would ever know where the oars were if whoever used the boat last took the oars home with him?"

Our minds came back to our appetites when from Poetry's place their five-minute dinner bell rang. There was also the sound of a car starting up near the mouth of the branch, which meant that Joe Sanders's tire was changed and he might get to Theodore Collins's mailbox before Theodore Collins's son did.

"Come over as soon after supper as you can," Poetry said as we separated. "And don't forget to bring a gunnysack for the frogs. And wear your sneakers so we won't get our feet cut on rocks while we're wading around. And bring your flashlight."

So away we went, he in his direction, and I in mine—Theodore Collins's first and worst son pedaling fast to try to catch up with Joe

Sanders so that I could be there when Mom opened the letter from Palm Tree Island and also the package, to see what was in it.

The mailman's red-white-and-blue truck had already stopped at our place and gone on. It was as far as the twin hickory nut trees on the way to Pony Ward's when I came pedaling up to our mailbox. Dad and Mom were standing under the plum tree, Dad holding the package from Palm Tree Island and Mom reading the letter, when I came through the gate.

My curiosity was ordering me to ask, "Anything special from Palm Tree Island, such as a letter or a package?" But I didn't.

Mom, who had been reading out loud, handed the letter to Dad. Then she began shuffling through the other letters to see if there was anything important enough to read next, as Charlotte Ann came toddling toward us from the grape arbor where she had been sitting in the shade cuddling her new twin dolls.

And then Old Man Paddler's secretary sniffed toward the kitchen and exclaimed, "Oh, my land of Goshen! Something's been on the stove too long!"

With that, Mom took off on the run toward the kitchen door so that whatever it was that was burning—if it was—could be saved.

Dad started whistling under his reddish brown mustache. He folded the letter Mom had handed to him and he had been listening to, took a deep breath, sighed, and said, "I hope you appreciate your mother, Son. When I married her, I didn't have any idea she would be such a good cook. I thought maybe a girl that had been a secretary for so many years, and a schoolteacher before that, might burn *everything* for the first few months. But, well, you haven't had any complaint, have you?"

There was such a friendly odor coming from the kitchen now that I let my curiosity about the mail from Palm Tree Island go to sleep in my mind and hurried to get washed up for lunch.

I had washed my hands at the grape arbor washbasin, dried them, and was at the screen door ready to open it and go in when I overheard Dad say, "Suppose I'd better telephone him?"

Guessing they were talking about Old Man Paddler, I said through the screen, "I got a card from him this morning. Joe gave it to me down at the branch bridge while he was waiting to get his tire fixed. What'd the letter from Palm Tree Island have in it? Anything special in the package? Any news about his twin brother?"

Dad looked quick at Mom.

She gave her head a mysterious shake, and then she said to me, "You want to come on in and finish setting the table? I typed right up to the last minute and almost forgot what time it was—the book is so interesting." Then Mom started humming the tune of a song that Little Jim's mother plays on the organ at all the funerals we have in Sugar Plain Church. It is on page 129 in our hymnal and begins:

Beyond the sunset, O blissful morning,
When with our Saviour heav'n is begun.

At the table we talked about different things, but most of the time, even though my mind was full of excitement about our new business venture, it seemed my folks had a secret that their first and worst son wasn't supposed to know about. The package, I noticed, wasn't anywhere in sight, and I wondered where it had gone so fast.

An idea hit me then. "Did they find Old Man Paddler's brother?" I asked. "Is he all right? When is he coming back to Sugar Creek? What did the letter say?"

"Not so fast and so many questions at once," Dad said, stopping me. Then he added, using an indifferent tone of voice and looking at Mom while he was talking to me, "One of the mission workers found him at the foot of a cliff, and he . . . well . . ." Then Dad looked at Mom again, got another mysterious look back, and finished, "He'd had a bad fall, and—" Dad stopped as if he wanted for some reason to change the subject, but then he went on. "The letter had a special message in it for Old Man Paddler. That's one reason why we think we'd better telephone him rather than just forward the letter to him. By the way, did you boys find your boat in good condition?"

That changed the subject, and even though I wasn't satisfied, it seemed I would have to wait for more information about the twin brother of Old Man Paddler.

Dad, who teaches the Homebuilder's Bible Class in our church, had the Bible on the table beside him open to Luke 15. Looking across at Mom, who was stirring the sugar she had just spooned into her cup of tea, he said, "If they had published *The Sugar Creek Times* in New Testament days, the shepherd who had a hundred sheep and lost one could have run an ad in the lost and found column, and the whole neighborhood would have started looking for it."

Mom, being a mother and a housekeeper as well as a part-time secretary, said, "And if the woman in that chapter who had ten coins and lost one had been a better housekeeper, she wouldn't have had to sweep the house first to find it."

"Also," I joined in to remark, "if early that morning, her son had washed all the downstairs windows for her"—which I myself had done at our house—"she wouldn't have had to light a candle so she could see the coin shining on the floor or wherever it was she finally found it."

Dad, who never likes to have anybody interrupt him when he is explaining something from the Bible or making a speech at a Farm Bureau convention, waved both arms around like a boy who has had his tent fall in on him and is trying to work his way up and out so that he can breathe. With a twinkle in his eyes at Mom, he accused us, "Words—words—words! You smother me with them. Let me finish."

We let him, and he and Mom discussed next week's Sunday school lesson while I asked to be excused and went out onto the side porch to look through *The Sugar Creek Times* and see if anything new had happened in the neighborhood.

I looked again at the big three-columns-wide, six-inches-deep ad featuring the Bay Tree Inn menu, wondering why we would get paid only fifty cents for a pair of frogs legs when they were going to charge so much more for a frogs legs dinner. I thought, *Maybe we ought to go on strike for higher wages*.

One item on page two of the *Times* had an Australian dateline. It told about a woman who walked into a tavern, emptied a box of ashes on the bar, and said, "Here he is—all that's left of him. You wanted him here all the time, and he was here every night. So take him, and good riddance!" And it was the cremated remains of her dead husband!

Another news story was about a boy named Darrel Inwood who had run away from home two weeks ago and hadn't been found. The sheriff and residents of Montgomery County had been looking for him all up and down the creek, thinking maybe he had drowned. But nobody had found him. His mother was "almost frantic," because he had been running around town with a motorcycle gang and several times had threatened to run away.

I didn't get to finish the news item because, from up the road in the direction of Pony Ward's place, there was the sound of a motorcycle again, coming at what looked and sounded like sixty miles an hour. It was stirring up a long cloud of gray white dust that went boiling out across our cornfield. As far as I could see up the road, there was dust and dust and more dust.

From behind me, Mom exclaimed, "Quick, Bill! Run upstairs and close the north window!"

Before I was able to get into the kitchen and through it and halfway up the stairs, I could hear Old Man Paddler's secretary closing the downstairs just-washed north windows to keep the road dust out of a good housekeeper's house.

I was at the upstairs window, closing it, when the motorcycle with two long-haired, red-jacketed riders on it went roaring past, pulling after them a trail of dust as dense as gray fog on a dark and humid Sugar Creek night.

Before going downstairs again, I noticed that the clothes closet door was open, and I saw, sitting on the top shelf, a brown box the size and shape of the package I had first seen in Joe Sanders's mail truck. I was standing and thinking and looking at it when I heard Dad's voice downstairs going on about his Sunday school lesson, as if the motorcycle with two boys on it wasn't any more than a fly buzzing around his mind and he could shoo it away with a wave of his hand.

When I went back down, Mom was at the table again, and Dad was right where he had been, the Bible still open at Luke 15 and his teacher voice saying, "As I was just explaining before my class left me, the *shepherd* went after the lost sheep, the *woman* searched for the lost coin, but no one went after the lost son. The prodigal had to get fed up with the disgusting life he was living, had to get sick at heart and homesick and ashamed. He had to learn the hard way that the way of the transgressor is hard. Then and only then did he come home. That's the law of life. That's the way it is."

"The way it is, yes," Mom said, "but the boy hadn't any business sinking all the way down to his neck in the hog wallow. Peter was smarter. When he was making such a fizzle of trying to walk on the water, he didn't wait until he had sunk all the way down. The Bible says, '*Beginning* to sink,' he called on the Lord to save him."

Mom was on her feet now, with hurrying in her mind. "If you and Bill want to help a working mother keep her house clean enough to drop a coin in without it getting lost, maybe you could clear the table for me. If Seneth decides to come right home, I'd like to have his manuscript finished. Strange, isn't it, that at a time like this he should have just completed a book on *The Christian After Death.*"

Mom stopped, as though she had been

driving too fast and had slammed on the brakes. "Whatever am I talking about, anyway?"

And now, for some reason, the fog in my mind was thicker than ever. From what Mom had just said, and had interrupted herself before finishing, it seemed that if I could just read the letter from Palm Tree Island it might say that they had not only found Kenneth Paddler and taken him to the hospital but that he had died. And my folks were going to telephone Old Man Paddler in California to see if maybe he would want to fly down to Palm Tree Island for the funeral.

Dad must have decided his class had really walked out on him, because he arose from the table, carried the Bible into the living room, and laid it on the table by the north window. From where he was, I heard him call, "Who closed all the windows in this house? Don't you know it's stuffy in here?"

Both Mom and I knew why the windows happened to be closed, but Dad didn't know, because he had been walking around in the pasture of his mind looking for a lost sheep.

Just then we heard the sound of the motorcycle again, this time from the *other* side of the house.

Looking away out across our south pasture toward Harm Groenwold's place, I saw a cloud of dust and a streak of shining cycle zooming up the lane. Then the motorcycle slowed down and skidded to a stop at the gate that led into Harm's cow pasture. One of the riders got off, swung open the gate, and climbed back on the motorcycle. Away the two went again toward the woods on the other side—out across the field, mind you, *leaving the gate open*—not wide open but wide enough for a boy or a cow to squeeze through.

4

Harm's old red bull!" Dad exclaimed. "He'll get out and run wild all over the county!"

With that, the teacher of the Homebuilders Bible Class was off like a two-legged bullet past the pitcher pump, through the barnyard, and over the pasture bars on the way to shut Harm Groenwold's gate so that Harm wouldn't have to go looking all over for a lost red bull.

I went to the kitchen to look for a towel to help dry the dishes Mom was already busy washing. The towel, for some reason, never managed to get lost but was always right there where it was supposed to be.

"Your father," Mom said, "is a remarkable man. He may have his few faults, but he is the finest husband a woman ever had. He was such a dreamer when I married him that I thought he might never be practical enough to get his work done. But I'd rather have him than any other man in the world. When you grow up, I hope you'll be as kind and gentle as he is. And as thoughtful of your wife.

"I was sorry the dust interrupted his lesson," Mom went on. "He was going to explain, I think, that the coin the woman lost was *not* out in the world somewhere but was *inside* the house, just like there are some lost people in the church or in the family who don't even know they are lost. We have to look for and find them too. Your father thinks the woman who sweeps the house reminds us of God's Holy Spirit, and the candle makes us think of the light of the gospel."

The phone rang then, and it was Dragonfly's mother, who had one of her many worries to talk over with Mom. So I got to finish the dishes alone. I was outdoors oiling the lawn mower only a few feet from the telephone window when I happened to hear Mom say through the now *open* window:

"It's not what this world is coming to, Thelma, it's what it has *already* come to. You know what the old hymn says—'The whole world was lost in the darkness of sin.' Most of those long-haired, sloppy-dressed, shiftless boys and girls are just *lost,* that's all. I feel so sorry for them, because they seem to like it that way . . . Yes, that's one of the worst things about it, the habits they take on . . . But what'll they be like ten years from now? They can't spend *all* of their lives floating around with their minds in a stupor! . . . Oh, *no!*" Mom all of a sudden exclaimed to Mrs. Gilbert. "That *is* going too far. Just wait until Theodore hears about that!"

She quickly put down the phone, hurried through the kitchen to the back door, and let out a long, quavering high-pitched call like a screech owl crying in the night, which is the way she calls the foreman of the jury when she wants to know what some verdict is.

"What's the matter?" I asked her.

She answered, "Those shiftless kids are stealing gasoline now! At Turkey Run State Park they left a spigot running, and the whole gas tank was empty this morning. If anyone had accidentally dropped a lighted match or a cigarette stub, half the cottages would have burned!"

Dad let Mom know he had heard her screech-owl wail by blowing a blast with the referee's whistle he carries on a string around his neck. He quickly closed Harm's gate, hurried across the lane that separates our two farms, swung himself over our fence, and half ran back across our south pasture to see what Mom had on her mind.

It was what was on *my* mind that seemed most important right then, though. *What*, I kept wondering as I followed the mower back and forth across the lawn, was in the letter from the missionary, and what mystery was in the little brown box in our upstairs closet? What was so important that my parents thought they ought to telephone Old Man Paddler about it?

My curiosity was so strong that, when I had finished another round-trip with the mower, I decided to stop and ask my folks an important question. I said first, standing near the iron pitcher pump, where they were at the time, "Am I a part of this family, and do I rate well enough to know what is going on? Some boys grow long hair and leave *home* because they feel they don't belong to the family."

Dad looked at me, gave my head a friendly swish of the hair on the back of my neck, and said, "You *do* need a haircut. We could run into town tonight, if you like, or maybe you'd rather go frog hunting."

My mother, who sometimes—in fact, quite often—helps Dad make up his mind about something, said to me, "The jury has reached a verdict. You do have a right to know. After all, you did spend a week in Palm Tree Island, you *did* find Kenneth Paddler, and you *are* a special friend of his twin brother. The letter says that not only did they find Kenneth Paddler lying at the foot of a cliff where he had fallen, and where he had lain for a week without food and water, but after they took him to the hospital, he died.

"One thing our dear Old Man Paddler will be glad to hear was that his brother died trusting in the Savior for the salvation of his soul. Kenneth's one heartache was that he hadn't come home soon after you boys found him. But it took him so long to regain his full mind after so many years of amnesia. When he did fully come to himself, he remembered he had been a newspaper reporter, so he decided to study the customs of the people and maybe even write a book about the plant and animal life of the island. He was far back in the interior when he had the accident.

"His dying request was that he be buried in

the old Sugar Creek cemetery on Strawberry Hill, where his parents and Sarah Paddler and his two nephews are buried—"

Mom's voice choked, and she let Dad finish.

"There wasn't any way to ship the body home," he said. "So, after getting permission from the government, they had the remains cremated. The little box upstairs, Son, contains the ashes of our dear Old Man Paddler's twin brother."

My father's voice sounded as if it had tears in it, and for a few minutes nobody said a word. But Nature's voices went right on. The hens in the barnyard kept on scratching and eating and singing. A meadowlark let out a cheerful jumble of juicy notes from somewhere up near the pignut trees. And from the woods across the road, a raspy-voiced crow called out a sad, funeral-like *"Caw-caw-caw-haw!"*

From the grape arbor where Charlotte Ann was in her small rocker, cuddling her twin dolls, there came her own tiny voice singing to them, "Sleep, baby, sleep. Thy Father is watching the sheep."

Mom found her voice again and said, "Maybe that's our answer. Our heavenly Father is watching His sheep."

Dad, with his arm around her to let her know her husband too was watching over and was going to take care of his wife, who was also my wonderful mother, said, "It's not going to be easy telling Seneth, but it has to be done."

With that, my father turned to go into the

house to the telephone, while I, his son, stood for a few minutes beside my mother.

I hardly realized I was doing what I was doing until I had done it, but my left arm went where Dad's arm had been only a few minutes before. "It's all right, Mom," I said to her. "We'll all stick together. I'll never let myself be a prodigal son—never. You want a drink?"

As soon as I had finished handing her a cup of fresh, clear water, which I had just pumped for her, I took a drink myself and tossed half a cup over the water trough, where it landed in the puddle there. As they always do, all the white and yellow butterflies that had been drinking around the border of the puddle took off in excited fluttering circles. Some of them loped toward the garden, others toward the blue morning glories swaying on their long vines at the grape arbor, where Charlotte Ann was sitting in the shade. But most of them settled back down around the pool where they had been—being still thirsty maybe.

"Beautiful, aren't they?" Mom said. And when I didn't answer because for some reason the tears my parents had had in their voices had gotten into mine, she added, "But they weren't *always* beautiful. In the larva stage, they were only little green or white caterpillars."

My mother's voice trailed away, and it seemed maybe she was thinking about Kenneth Paddler again.

I knew she was when her mind seemed to come back from wherever it was and she said,

"I must get back to the typewriter." And she left me and went into the house, where Dad was trying to place a long-distance call to Old Man Paddler in California. I thought the old man might be out on the barge in the Pacific Ocean fishing again for mackerel.

Never in all my life before had I had a feeling like the one that was hurting my heart right that minute. The little brown box upstairs was all that was left of Kenneth Paddler, the man who, when he was a boy, used to play right here in our own territory, up and down and in Sugar Creek. He probably ran *lickety-sizzle* through the woods with bare feet, listening to the birds singing and watching the flying squirrels take off on long, slanting leaps, riding the air from the trees to the ground. He had fished in all the best places. He had gone to the Sugar Plain Church, which, that many years ago, Old Man Paddler had told us, was only a small log building without even a steeple. But now he had gone beyond the sunset, and all that was left of his life here was a little box of ashes.

Charlotte Ann all of a sudden got tired of rocking her dolls. She came over to the pump platform where I still was, saying up to me, "I'm thirsty."

I looked down at her reddish brown hair and into her blue eyes, as blue as the morning glories at the grape arbor, and said to her, calling her by the new name our family had been calling her for the past several weeks, "Don't worry, Honey Girl. Your brother will always look after you. Promise me you'll never be a prodigal girl?"

Her answer was, "Honeybee Girl is thirsty!"

"Not Honeybee Girl," I corrected her. "Just Honey Girl."

I took her little pink plastic drinking cup from the wire hook on the pump, filled it, and handed it to her.

But instead of drinking it, she tossed the water over the tank into the puddle, saying as she did it, "Peanut butterflies thirsty!"

"Not peanut butterflies," I corrected her, "just butterflies."

And do you know what? That little reddish-brown-haired sister of mine proved she was a member of the Collins family and a sister of her brother by getting a set expression in her eyes as she looked up at me, shook her head, and answered, "*Peanut* butterflies!" Then she took off in the direction of the garden, chasing one of the yellow peanut butterflies that had been drinking with the white ones a few seconds before, and I went into the house.

As I stopped in the kitchen, listening for a minute to Mom's typewriter keys flying along on Old Man Paddler's book, *The Christian After Death,* part of a poem we had to memorize in school went fluttering around in my mind:

> *Life is real, life is earnest*
> *And the grave is not its goal;*
> *Dust thou art, to dust returnest*
> *Was not spoken of the soul.*

It was after supper but still daylight when Dragonfly came biking up to "Theodore Collins" on our mailbox. Tonight was the night when the Thompson, Gilbert, and Collins Frogs Legs Supply Company would hold their grand opening. Mom was at the organ at the time, playing and singing a hymn. She sometimes took time to do that, even when there was a lot of work to be done.

"In business offices," I had heard her once explain to Dad, "they have a coffee break. It gives all the workers a chance to relax for a few minutes and pick up a little energy. As a busy housewife and mother, I find a *hymn* break absolutely necessary now and then."

Having heard her say that to Dad, I had said, "There are times, too, when your son needs a *fishing* break. It gives him a chance to pick up a lot of energy he loses weeding the garden."

The hymn my mother was playing and also singing loud enough for me to hear, but not loud enough for Dragonfly at our front gate to hear, was one we had in our new church hymnal. It goes:

Have you come to the Red Sea place in
    your life,
Where in spite of all you can do,
There is no way out, there is no way back,
There is no other way but through?

As I left the window and raced out to meet Dragonfly, it seemed I ought to pray for Old

Man Paddler, who had come to a Red Sea place in *his* life, and there wasn't any way out or back. He would *have* to go through with the funeral of his twin brother, Kenneth. Even as I ran, I heard myself saying, "Let him know how much You love him, and help him all the way through. Help the gang to be extra kind to him and to all old people."

In a few minutes Dragonfly and I were on our bikes, pedaling as fast as we could into our new venture, not knowing we were going to stumble onto another little brown box the size and shape of the one sitting on the top shelf of the closet of the Collins upstairs north room.

We waited at Poetry's guest house until dark, which came a lot sooner than it sometimes does, because low gray clouds had begun to move in from the west. There was the feel of rain in the air, and it was already beginning to mist a little.

"Perfect weather for frogs," Poetry said, shining his flashlight down the gravel road toward the branch bridge. "On a night like this, the frogs are very happy. Hear those tree frogs down in the swamp? They like damp weather."

I listened in the direction of the swamp, the sycamore tree, and the cave, which is the back passageway to the basement of Old Man Paddler's cabin. And it seemed the tree frogs might be having some kind of national frog celebration, there were so many of them.

But it was the bullfrogs I was especially

interested in. It sounded as though there were maybe a hundred great big luggers all up and down the creek but especially over on the island where, in a little while, we would begin harvesting them for the Bay Tree Inn Dining Room.

As we rambled down the hill, our sneakers made little crunching noises on the road like baby bullfrogs with gravelly voices just learning to talk frog language.

Poetry, ahead of me, stopped so suddenly I bumped into him. "Did you ever in all your life see so many fireflies?" he asked.

"It would take a lot of spiders to eat all of them," I remarked and maybe shouldn't have.

"As I was beginning to say before you tried to change the subject," Poetry answered me, "the *Photinus pyralis*—that's Latin for firefly—has only a short while to live after it becomes an adult."

My almost best friend's voice took on a teacher tone as he talked, like my father's voice when he talks about prodigal sons, lost coins, and straying sheep. "Science has been experimenting with fireflies, catching them and storing them in a deep freeze. In one experiment they put four hundred of them in test tubes in a dark room at seventeen degrees below zero for three years. And when the three years were up, they looked at all those dead *Photinus pyralis* in the dark, and they still gave off a greenish light."

Our sneakers were still making their gravel-voiced *scrunch, scrunch, scrunchety-scrunch* in the road. In only a little while we would come to the branch bridge, take off down the incline, and follow the lilac hedge to the boat.

"Also," Poetry's teacher voice went on, "science may someday discover that the energy that turns on and off the fireflies' flashlights is *very* important. Already they know that it is caused by the oxidation of something called luciferin, which is Latin for 'to bring light.'"

"You must have spent all afternoon reading your science magazine," I said to Poetry. "But do you know that the name *Lucifer* was the first name the Devil had?" And then my own voice took on a teacher tone as I quoted something I had heard my father say once. "Lucifer is back of all the meanness there is in the world, and the reason for all the darkness—not *light*—is because people let him run their lives the way he wants to."

But it was as if Poetry's mind was still wading around in the science magazine Joe Sanders had left at their house that morning. *"Look!"* he whispered, as if he didn't want the lightning bugs to hear us and stop their performance. "Did you ever see so much luciferin in your life?"

Over on the island there were maybe ten thousand fireflies turning on and off their cold green lights and streaking here and there above the water like that many schoolboys writing with green chalk on a blackboard as big as an outdoors night. They were making dots and dashes, question marks and exclamation points —and the blackboard was all around us and up and down the creek.

But it was the voices of the big luggers on the island that made the night seem more important.

Dragonfly startled us then. He had been quiet most of the time while Poetry and I were telling each other how much we knew. "Some of the fireflies have awful *big* lights," he said. "Like maybe they are giants!"

And that's when Poetry and I came to. We stopped stock-still and stared.

"Flashlights!" Poetry decided out loud, just as I decided the same thing in my mind.

"Somebody else has started a frogs legs company. Somebody else saw the ad in the *Times* and is going to sell frogs legs, too!"

Dragonfly, who had maybe read stories or heard programs about the Old West and gold mining, burst out, "Somebody's jumped our claim. Come on! Let's get the boat and row over and stop 'em!"

Before either Poetry or I *could* have stopped him, that little rascal of a junior member of the Thompson, Gilbert, and Collins Company took off ahead of us on the run for the path that leads from the branch bridge to the boat.

Poetry and I took off after that spindle-legged dumb-bunny member of our company to stop him. But he was like the lead dog of a pack of hounds on a hot coon trail as he sped down the road, his flashlight bobbing, his sneakers stirring up dust. Or else it was fog I was seeing, because the weather was beginning to get more humid, and fog was beginning to move across the road, floating in from the creek.

At the branch bridge, Dragonfly stopped, panting, and there he waited for us, as though his mind had begun to work again or else he was mixed up in his thoughts.

The minute I was near enough, I grabbed him and held on, ordering him, "Don't *ever* make a foolish move like that! You don't *know* that anybody has jumped our claim! That might be somebody fishing. And anybody has a right to fish anywhere along the creek he wants to."

But we decided to creep cautiously along the lilac hedge to our boat and keep on keeping as quiet as we could to see what was happening on the island.

5

My mind and muscles were tense, and I was even trembling a little, thinking about our boat having been moved. I whispered to Poetry, "Now we'll find out who's been borrowing our boat and what for."

I think I was disappointed when we got to where our boat was—it was still there and all right—for the pair of flashlights that had been making on-and-off flashes over on the island began moving toward the other shore, *not* toward ours.

We crouched there by our boat, the gunnysack beside us, our flashlights off, waiting, wondering what on earth and why, hoping for something. We didn't know what. And I was still trembling a little.

Dragonfly whispered close to my ear, "They're going on across. They're wading the riffle to Tom Till's side of the creek."

Poetry showed what kind of person he was when he said, "If it *is* Tom Till and his brother, Bob, and if they've been hunting frogs, it's all right. Their mother's been sick, and they need the money."

Even Dragonfly agreed when he said, "Tom's mother is an awful nice mother. She almost died after her last operation. And when my mother was sick, she sent her a get-well card."

In a little while the two boys—maybe men, but probably two boys—had waded across the narrow riffle to the shore on the other side of the island and disappeared in the cornfield in the direction of the Tills' house. And we decided it was time for us to start our first business venture—if there were any frogs left, which it seemed there were, because there was still a lot of bellowing going on over on the island.

Even though my mind kept seeing a little brown box on the top shelf in the Collins family closet, the sad thoughts got pushed back into a corner of my mind because of all the excitement we were about to row our boat into.

We hadn't been on the island more than a few minutes when the fog began to move in. It was not thick enough so that we couldn't see, but it was like walking around in a big white cloud every few minutes before the cloud would move on across the island or thin itself down to nothing for a while.

A few feet out from the island shore, we followed our flashlights along as they tunneled their way through the dark. A foot or two out from shore were scores of kidney-shaped mud plantain leaves floating on their long underwater stalks, and it was among these we would find our biggest frogs.

Every now and then one of us would spot the shining eyes of a big lugger and creep stealthily toward him with the flashlight focused on him—carefully, *very* carefully, slowly, *very* slowly working our way a little closer until the light would be only a few inches from his head. Then we'd reach a hand around behind him, make a quick grab, catch the green-nosed, long-hind-legged, gravel-voiced, tailless amphibian around his wide, flat backbone and hold on tight until we could plop him into the open mouth of the gunnysack. And we would have made another fifty cents.

For some reason, though—maybe because the Till boys had already caught or scared away some of our harvest—our business venture wasn't doing well. Even though we'd heard what sounded like seventy-seven monsters when we had still been at the top of Poetry's hill, after working what seemed a long time we had caught only seven, only $3.50 worth.

With Kenneth Paddler's ashes on my mind, and thinking how sad Old Man Paddler was going to be or already was because my father by now had surely made telephone connections to California—I was worried. I knew that pretty soon I would have to tell Poetry, just to get part of my mind's load unloaded onto his.

Dragonfly was having too much fun to be told anything sad. Besides, he was too superstitious and might think that Kenneth Paddler's spirit would also be in the box. Or maybe it had come back to Sugar Creek and was walking around on the island.

At any ordinary time, I would have enjoyed the sounds and sights that make a Sugar Creek night a lot more interesting than the world most grown-ups live in at night. Just once, as I waded around among the mud plantain leaves, I happened to think that the yellow dots on the pickerel weeds' violet blue flowers looked like hundreds of fireflies that had turned their lights on but didn't have enough oxidation to turn them off. Maybe when I got home I could tell my mother what I had happened to think, and it would give her a glad feeling in her mind because she liked nature so well.

And then, right in the middle of my mud-dle, about fifteen feet to my right, Dragonfly let out an excited: "Hey! I've found a hidden treasure!"

Poetry, the senior member of our company, who was maybe only seven feet to my left and near the boat, scared the daylights out of me by yelling past me to Dragonfly, "You found *what?*"

"A box full of gold and jewels and—and—and *everything!*"

With that excited answer, Dragonfly came splashing toward us, bringing with him a brown box *the same size and shape* as the one I had seen at home that afternoon on our upstairs closet shelf—the one addressed to Old Man Paddler and postmarked Palm Tree Island!

My mind was interrupted right then by the sound of wheels racing across the big Sugar Creek bridge about a quarter of a mile up-stream. When I took a quick look, the vehicle was all the way across and gone, so I brought my mind and eyes back to Dragonfly's treasure.

"My mother found an old horseshoe this morning, and I found five four-leaf clovers, and—" he began.

"*Sh!* Not so loud!" Poetry shushed our superstitious little friend. "Somebody might be watching!"

The three of us were in a little circle now, our flashlights focused on the box and on some odd-shaped letters, which could have been Chinese or maybe some other language.

"Where'd you find it?" Poetry asked, and in the reflected light I saw his face was serious. His jaw muscles were set, and his eyes were narrowed as if he was seeing not only the strange lettering on the box but seeing inside as well.

Dragonfly's answer came with a stutter. "R–r–right over there! B–b–buried in th–th–that drift! I s–s–saw that red ribbon, p–p–picked it up and p–p–pulled on it, and it was tied to this b–b–box."

Not only was there a four-or-five-foot-long red ribbon hanging from the box, but it was wrapped round and round and round in different directions with the same color ribbon.

If the box had been buried in a pile of drift from last spring's flood, it had maybe floated down from far upstream. But it might have been buried here for years and years, and the flood had unearthed it. And it might be very valuable, as Dragonfly had said.

I said my thoughts to Poetry, who was studying the strange lettering.

But he shook his head. "This box has never

been wet. It's as dry as if somebody had tucked it into this drift only a little while before we got here. The ribbon is also dry."

Then he let out a gasp. "*The flashlights!* We saw somebody moving around over here less than an hour ago."

Now Poetry was running his hand in and out of different pockets of his jeans. He came out with his little magnifying glass, which I knew he carried, and which, when we needed a match and didn't have any, could be used to start a fire with dead, decayed dry wood.

As Poetry studied the lettering on the box, he let out another quiet gasp. "Maybe we'll make *more* than three fifty tonight. Here—read this!"

He handed the magnifying glass to me, and this is what I saw in very small topsy-turvy printing: "For liberal reward, return to Mary Jane Moragrifa."

There wasn't any address.

As I stared at the little brown box with the woman's name on it, the weather in my mind was as misty as nature's weather was beginning to be. A dry box with a five-foot red ribbon on it, more red ribbon wrapped round and round it, Mary Jane Moragrifa's name on it, and a promised reward. It was like one of Grimm's fairytales.

Because the weather was getting to be still more foggy, making it hard to see, it seemed maybe we should close our business for the night and go home, taking the box with us.

Three dollars and fifty cents wasn't very much to earn, to be divided by three, but it was better than nothing. Besides, as Dragonfly right then said, "The reward might be as much as a hundred dollars—maybe even a thousand!"

We were in the boat, ready to start rowing toward the shore, when Poetry quieted us with a hiss. "*Psst!* You guys hear anything?"

I listened as hard as I could in every direction. I didn't hear anything except the maybe two hundred tree frogs having their national celebration, a few scattered bullfrogs bellowing, and other ordinary night sounds. I'd started to say so when I thought I did hear something from the direction of the branch bridge.

We squinted our eyes toward the mouth of the branch and the lilac hedge, every nerve tense, and I could feel every drop of blood in my body tingling. But as before, there were only the ordinary night sounds a boy can hear any night down along the creek—a beaver in the bayou making his dam stronger, night herons calling to each other, or maybe a screech owl letting loose with his quavering high-pitched wail, crying, "*Sha–a–a–a–y!*"

A screech owl did call out right then. And for a fleeting second it seemed there ought to be a referee's whistle answering it from our south pasture.

Well, after several minutes of tense waiting, we didn't hear anything suspicious, and we shoved off and rowed toward the shore.

As soon as our boat was tied to its sapling, we gathered ourselves into a circle again to have another and closer look at Dragonfly's find.

How, I wondered as I read, *could anybody return the box to anybody named Mary Jane Moragrifa if there wasn't any address or telephone number?*

Poetry turned the box over and over, having wrapped the five feet of ribbon around it and tucked it in under the knot of other ribbon so that it wouldn't drag on the ground and be stepped on when we carried it up to the Thompson guesthouse. What to do with the box would be a problem for us to work out after we got to Poetry's place, cleaned the frogs, and put the fourteen big fat frogs legs in their refrigerator.

"There's got to be something else written on this box," Poetry said, holding it closer to my flashlight and focusing his magnifying glass on all four sides. He startled us then with a whistle that had an exclamation point on it.

"What?" I gasped.

Dragonfly asked, "What?" with his actions, crowding in to see what Poetry's whistle seemed to say he had seen.

And then, before I could see what his magnifying glass had magnified, we were half scared out of what few wits we had at the time when from behind us there was a gravel-voiced bawl, like a calf learning to cry and getting stopped by somebody choking it.

I sighed a small sigh of relief when I found it was only Dragonfly himself. He had stepped on our gunnysack, and one of the frogs in bullfrog language had croaked, *"Ou–ou–ouch!"*

I'd started to look again through Poetry's magnifying glass when I got interrupted once more, this time by a flash of light up near the branch bridge. The light was going on, then off. On, then off.

Poetry whispered, "It's a car with only one headlight! I wonder if—" He stopped in the middle of his sentence. "We've got to get out of here *quick!* Follow me, you guys!"

He whirled, stumbling over the gunnysack of frogs. The little brown box with the red ribbon on it slipped out of his hands as he went down. Dragonfly shot in after it, scooped it up, and, in another shuffle of minutes, the Thompson, Gilbert, and Collins Frogs Legs Supply Company was running toward the path that follows the shore of the creek to the sycamore tree and the cave. It was the path that, if you keep on it, will lead you into the swamp, through it to Old Man Paddler's cabin, and still on to the haunted house.

It wasn't easy to be sure of our directions because of the fog. And the weather in my mind was getting even more foggy as I wondered what was going on and why. What was in the little brown box that was worth a liberal reward if found and returned to some woman or girl named Mary Jane Moragrifa? And what had Poetry seen with his magnifying glass?

Part of the answer to my worry was only another and worse worry.

From the bushes to our left a shadowy form shot out and grappled with Poetry. Down the two went right in front of me. I stumbled over them, and down I also went—and Dragonfly came tumbling after.

In that same flash of a second, another boy darted in from the fog, and there was a tangled-up scramble of ten arms, ten legs, and five minds.

Maybe the three of us could have licked the stuffings out of the two of them, even if they were a lot bigger, if it had been daylight and they had wanted to fight. But it seemed they didn't. What they wanted was Mary Jane Mora-grifa's little brown box.

"They st-st-stole my box!" Dragonfly cried from the ground behind me, and there was fiery temper in his voice. "Come on, you guys! We've got to catch 'em!"

And away we all went, pell-mell, *lickety-sizzle, crunch-crunchety-crunch.* Hurry, hurry, hurry. Worry, worry, worry. We were following our stolen property and maybe running headfirst into a fierce, fast fistfight that would get us bashed noses, whammed jaws, twisted arms—anything that can happen to a boy in a blind fight he maybe shouldn't be in but sometimes finds himself in the middle of before he knows it.

6

Even as I ran stumbling along, dodging bushes and leaping over logs, through the fog and the tall grass, I was remembering that the two who had attacked us and stolen the just found little brown box were a lot bigger than we were.

"Those *crazy girls!*" Poetry, running ahead of me, exclaimed in an angry voice.

"*Girls?*" I shouted up to him. "What makes you think they're girls?"

"Because," Poetry panted back over his shoulder, "I caught one of them by the hair and pulled some of it out, that's why."

Well, those two thieves—boys or girls or maybe one of each—were as fast as a couple of red foxes with three bloodthirsty hounds after them. If only we could get to that car and head them off . . .

But my thoughts were like soap bubbles bursting into nothing. There was the explosion of a starting motor ahead of us near the branch bridge, and a headlight was turned on—*one* headlight. It turned this way and that, making a wide circle, then back, and the motor leaped into faster thundering life.

"It's not a car! It's a *motorcycle!*" I cried to Poetry ahead of me and to Dragonfly behind me.

"Let's get the license number!" Poetry shouted.

I stumbled over a tree root right then and landed sprawling in the grass beside a sweet-smelling lilac bush. My mind was in a dizzying whirlwind of worry as I remembered another motorcycle I had seen and heard earlier in the day—one that had driven past our place at maybe sixty miles an hour and had had two long-haired riders on it. And that same motor-cycle had stormed up the lane on the south side of our place, going through the gate into Harm Groenwold's pasture and zooming out across that pasture toward Harm's woods, fol-lowing the branch in the direction of the Bay Tree Inn.

I scrambled to my feet, glad I had my sneakers on, so that my right big toe, which was a *little* sore, hadn't gotten maybe even broken.

I shook my head to shake out the muddle that was in it, just in time to see the thundering motorcycle race across the board-floored branch bridge and up the hill past Poetry's place and disappear in the foggy, foggy dew.

Now what? my mind asked me. And I didn't have any answer. What can three boys who have been robbed of a treasure worth maybe a thou-sand dollars to the owner and a liberal reward to us—what can those three boys do at a time like that! In the mixed-up rough-and-tumble scuffle, we had also lost $3.50 worth of frogs.

The fog was beginning to turn into misty rain now, and if we didn't get to Poetry's place in a hurry, we would get soaking wet. We wouldn't even have time to go back to where we had lost our frogs and look for them.

Grunting, panting out our disappointment, as mad as three wet hens, the Thompson, Gilbert, and Collins Frogs Legs Supply Company hurried up the gravel hill the motorcycle had gone racing up only a few minutes before.

The gang had been in a lot of mixed-up adventures in the past, some of them dangerous and filled with mystery, some of them the kind in which we had had to use our muscles and fists as well as our minds.

Several of those exciting times went fluttering through my thoughts as I scurried with the other members of our company up that hill. One of the most interesting and exciting times we had *ever* had was when we had gone on that vacation to Palm Tree Island. There we had found Old Man Paddler's long-lost twin brother, whose cremated remains were in a little brown box in a closet in our house. A box that was, I thought again, the size and shape of the one with Mary Jane Moragrifa's name printed on it, which was right now on the flying motorcycle.

It certainly was a foggy night in my mind, I happened to think as the three of us reached the top of the hill and were ready to turn in at the Thompsons' gate. There Poetry stopped us with an idea.

"Listen—we may have lost our frogs and maybe a hundred-dollar reward, but we *can* go back and look for the frogs. What if we *do* get wet? It wouldn't be the first time! But what's *more* important, we don't have to lose the reward either. All is not lost as long as there are nine of us. We *can* do something about it!"

"Nine!" I moaned my disappointment, feeling drops of rain on my face right then. It certainly wasn't the time for any of us to try to be funny.

"Nine altogether," he said. "Remember the poem I gave in that reading at the Sugar Creek Literary Society last week? The one by Nixon Waterman?"

What, I thought, could a poem by somebody named Nixon Waterman, quoted last week by Leslie Thompson at a literary society meeting, do to help us get back our stolen property, worth maybe a hundred dollars to us and a thousand to Mary Jane Moragrifa?

We were at Poetry's spirea hedge now. "You guys wait right here until I get my flash camera," he said. "We've got to go back down and take a picture of those tire marks where the motorcycle was standing." And away our roly-poly friend went toward his house, his flash-light tunneling through the fog to lead the way for him.

When Poetry didn't come back out right away, Dragonfly began to get worried. "Why isn't he back? What's taking him so long?"

"Listen!" I shushed my worrying friend, for I heard Poetry talking to somebody about something. We didn't have much time to wonder to whom about what before he was back out where we were, his flash camera in one hand and his flashlight in the other.

"What took you so long?" Dragonfly wanted to know.

He got an evasive answer. "I had to make a phone call. I'll tell you about it later. Now, about the Waterman poem. In case you have forgotten, it says that nobody is all alone when he stands between the two best friends he has ever known. And those two best friends, the poem's last line says, 'are his two good honest hands.'

"That means that the three of us, having two good honest hands apiece, have six best friends to help us. And that makes *nine* altogether, as against four *bad, dishonest* hands of two thieves. We also have two and a half good minds," Poetry finished.

I couldn't help but ask, "And which one of us has only half a mind?" It seemed he had only about half a mind himself right that minute.

"I," Poetry agreed with my thoughts, "have only half a mind left. I gave that girl I had the fight with a piece of it."

We had talked too long already. Action was needed and in a hurry. Poetry held out his right best friend, palm up, and barked to us, "It'll be raining hard in a few minutes. If we don't get the pictures, the tracks will be washed out. Come on! Follow me!"

In a few minutes we were back at the bridge. Finding a clear, sharp tread mark, Poetry focused his camera on it, snapped the flash picture, and straightened up, listening in the direction of the Theodore Collins place as if he was expecting to hear something. "They ought to be here any minute now."

"Who?" I wanted to know.

"I phoned the sheriff and told him what had happened and where—listen!"

I strained my ears in the direction of the Collins place, which is the direction Sheriff Jim Colbert and his posse would be coming from if they came.

And that's when from the *opposite* direction, from over the crest of the hill, there came the *splat-splat-splat br-r-r-r-r* of the motorcycle again. Now its headlight came bob-bob-bobbing down toward us on the washboard gravel road.

At such a time there is only one thing to do, and all nine of us did it. We went down that embankment like that many bullfrogs trying to get out of the way of a boy's flashlight and scrambled like scared cottontails for the shelter of the lilac hedge.

It was a ridiculous time to think what I happened to think right then, but I thought of the story we had read in school when we were younger about a frog who thought he was very brave—braver than any other frog in the world. He wasn't even afraid of a cow with long horns, he said. He was bragging on himself to a school of smaller frogs, saying, "All I have to do when the cow with the long horns comes thundering toward me is to puff myself out until I am as big as the cow herself. And the cow will get scared and run away." Just then, the story goes, an old cow broke through the fence and scared the bragging frog half to death. He took a fast headfirst leap into the frog pond and never talked again about being brave. Which proves it's never a good idea to brag on yourself.

In another minute the motorcycle with whoever was on it would go flying across the bridge, up the hill on the other side to the north road, on to the Theodore Collins place, on and still on, and maybe run into the sheriff's roadblock. From the lilacs, we could see without being seen.

But do you know what? That motorcycle slowed down and skidded to a stop at the bridge. They shut off the motor but left the headlight on, using it like a spotlight, turning the handlebars this way and that, lighting up the whole area. Only the lilacs we were behind kept us from being seen.

What if they spotted us? And what would they want with us anyway? They already had what they had been after.

I could hear them talking with disgruntled voices to each other, walking all around where our battle had been, using their flashlights now. One of the boys had a higher-pitched voice than the other, which made me think he might be a lot younger.

They were getting close to our hiding place, and I heard one of them say as plain as day, "It's got to be right over there by the lilacs where I had the scuffle with the chunky boy. He not only knocked it off, but he took a handful of hair with it!"

One of the boys was swearing, calling us different kinds of names. If I had happened to have less good sense than courage, that would have sent me flying out of my shelter into a red-haired temper explosion. But at a time like that, a bragging bullfrog would be smarter to stay out of the way of a cow—and let anybody who wanted to, think he was a coward.

The three of us were in such a close huddle we could hear each other breathing. I could also hear my heart pounding.

I was startled half out of my wits right then when one of them began swishing the lilac bushes this way and that, only a few feet from us!

"Right here!" he called to the other one. "It's got to be right here somewhere! If I don't find it, Oliver will half kill me and then make me go home. *I can't go home!*"

There came back the deeper, older-sounding voice, disagreeing and also scolding. "Will you stop blubbering! We can't stay here all night. I'll take care of Oliver for you. We've got the box, and that's all that's really important!"

And that's when the lilacs, which had been having an unseen battle with Dragonfly's nose, won the battle. Dragonfly sneezed.

That's also when Dragonfly's mind exploded him into action. Maybe it was his sneeze, which he knew had given him away, or else it was the mention of the little box that he had found and they had stolen. He was out of our hiding place quicker than a firefly's fleeting flash. That little junior member of the Thompson, Gilbert, and Collins Frogs Legs Supply Company leaped like a spindle-legged frog toward the boy who had the box. He dived headfirst into him, grappled him around the ankles, and the battle for the box was on.

The battle for the box was not only on, but it looked for a minute as though it was going to be a battle for *life* for that fiery little fistfighter.

Then I guess Poetry remembered something I had forgotten—the pledge of allegiance the three of us had made when we organized our company, especially that part of it that said "Until death do us part." He quoted it, half to me and half to himself, just before the two of us went flying out into the arena where the junior member of our company was about to get the daylights knocked out of him.

But believe it or not, that skinny little member of our firm still had his man down and was holding onto one of his legs like a bulldog, accusing him, "You're a thief! You stole my box of jewelry, and it's *mine!* You're going to give it back! *Help! Help! H–E–L–P!*" he called to Poetry and me.

At a time like that, you don't have time to think what a dumb-bunny thing the junior member of your company has done and is doing. You hear him calling for help. You see the big lummox he is fighting with right that very minute whamming your much smaller friend with a fist as big and maybe as hard as a prizefighter's. Now he began hitting at Dragonfly with the box itself, using it as a weapon while he held onto it by the red ribbon that was wrapped around it.

Until death do us part! I exclaimed to myself.

The other boy must have been using his mind as well as his muscles. From the other side of where we had been, I heard him yell, "Be careful of that box! It's worth a lot of money! Don't let 'em get it. Quick! Throw it to me!"

I was still in the thick of things when I saw Dragonfly's man, who was now on his back, suddenly toss the box over his shoulder toward the lilac hedge. It went sailing through the air with the greatest of ease. The ribbon that was tied around it and the extra length of ribbon that had come loose were dangling from it like a kite's tail.

Also flying up into the air, with not quite so much ease, was a heavyset boy named Leslie Poetry Thompson. What he was doing was more prose than poetry as, three feet up in the air, he intercepted that backward pass.

Dragonfly, not knowing what was happening behind his back, was still holding on for dear life to the leg of the boy he had tackled. Poetry was dodging this way and that, trying to get away from the second big lummox. And I, Theodore Collins's first and very worst son, was in the middle of everything but not sure just where.

Knowing I was pledged to do something until death do us part, I turned myself into a cow with horns and raced toward the stomach of the tough who was trying to get the box away from Poetry.

If you have ever had anybody hit you with a hard head in the middle of your stomach and had the wind so knocked out of you that you couldn't breathe, that was maybe what I had just done to the ruffian I had right that minute rammed into. He let out a yell, doubled up, and that part of the battle was history.

At the same time, Poetry yelled, "Come on, Bill! Dragonfly! Let's get out of here!"

And out of there we got, as soon as Dragonfly could get untangled from his man. In less than almost no time, the three of us—or was it all *nine* of us—were racing toward the creek and the path we knew led to the cave.

In only seconds we were away from the long cone of light from the motorcycle's headlight and into the five thousand flashing lights of that many fireflies, all of us running in the rain like three cottontails with two mad dogs after them. And the bunnies, which we ourselves were, knew the territory, and the mad dogs didn't.

7

In all our scuffle with the ruffians, the thieves, Sons of Lucifer, the Devil's angels, or whatever they were, Poetry had been smart enough to keep his flashlight in his pocket. So we would have it to use when we got to the cave, which Poetry decided was where we were going.

"How come the cave?" I managed to ask as we ran, dodging weeds and water puddles in the path.

"Because it's closer than my place now, and we've got to get somewhere fast. Those Devil's angels are not angels, you know. We don't know *what* they'd do to us if they ever caught us again."

"Maybe they know about the cave!" Dragonfly managed to say. "They're f–f–following us!"

And the two were. A flashlight was bobbing behind us and, in spite of the tumbling water in the riffle beside us as we ran, I imagined I could hear the *plop–plop–plop* of angry feet thundering toward us like the thundering hooves of Harm Groenwold's old red bull when he is mad at something or other out in the south pasture.

If we could get to the cave first, and into it, and maybe through it to the basement of Old

Man Paddler's cabin, we could quickly lock the door, dive up the cellar stairway, go through the trapdoor into the house, and be safe.

In the cabin, I knew, was a telephone that had an unlisted number, which only a few people knew—mostly just the members of the gang and their folks—because, while the old man was writing his book, he had had too many calls to interrupt his mind.

Now we were at the sycamore tree and the incline that led up to the cave's wide mouth. Up we scrambled, and in we went. There we shushed ourselves into silence, keeping Poetry's flashlight off.

We hadn't been in the cave's outer room more than a few minutes before the rough, tough guys who had been chasing us were at the base of the sycamore tree below. We dropped down to keep from being seen, because their flashlight began searching all around everywhere, up to and past the cave's entrance and down the winding path that goes into the swamp.

"No tracks here," one of them said. "I'll bet they're up there in the cave." He shot a long beam straight up to where I had been peeking over the edge, and I had to duck down like a bullfrog dunking himself to get out of sight of a flashlight.

"All right!" One of the boy's voices barked savagely like a policeman's voice giving an order to a hiding fugitive. "Throw down the box, and we'll let you go!"

That's when Poetry whispered to us a short, sharp order. "Let's go!"

And away the three members of the Thompson, Gilbert, and Collins Frogs Legs Supply Company went, hurrying through the familiar cave passageway we knew so well. Turning to the left here. To the right there. Slipping through one narrow place after another. Into one large or smaller room after another. Up and up and up. Always up. We knew that in just a little while we'd be at the big wooden door to the old man's cellar. And soon we were.

While Poetry was fumbling around in the secret place where the key was kept, we stopped —*got stopped,* rather.

"*Sh!*" Dragonfly hissed. "Listen! The old man's phone's ringing!"

And it was. As plain as you can hear a phone ringing through a heavy wooden door, up a stairway, and through a trapdoor at the top, there was the honest-to-goodness faraway sound of the ringing of a telephone!

"Must be somebody who doesn't know he's in California," Dragonfly suggested.

Poetry startled us with: "Or it might be Mary Jane Moragrifa!"

The idea was so surprising that I wondered, *What on earth?* and said so.

"*That,*" Poetry came back with, "is what I saw with the magnifying glass. The old man's unlisted number—447-3132."

Now we were in an even deeper mystery than we had been. Whoever had lost the box could be somebody who knew the unlisted number of the telephone that right this minute was still ringing!

How long the phone had been ringing, we didn't know. If nobody answered it—and I didn't see how anybody could unless he was in the cabin—it would stop.

Then Poetry let out a groan. "Oh, no!"

"Oh, no, *what?*" I asked.

His voice was muffled a little by all the nervous searching of his hand on the secret shelf where the key was kept. But what Poetry *said* was as clear as a school bell.

"The key is gone!"

He hadn't any sooner said that than from far back in the passageway there was a flash of light. And I knew from the kind of light it was—and how strong it was—that it wasn't any firefly oxidizing his luciferin. That light was as bright as a hundred dozen lightning bugs in a huddle, turning on all their lights at the same time and leaving them on.

At that same second we heard footsteps and knew that the two who had lost the first round of their battle to get back the box of jewels, or whatever was in it, hadn't given up or been thrown off the track. They had followed us into the cave and all the way through it. And right that very minute they were about to come into the last long room, at this end of which we ourselves were. They were coming toward the big, closed cellar door—the big closed and *locked* cellar door!

In a situation like that, there isn't any time to think about a song you've heard your mother playing and singing, but the words and the tune were in my mind anyway, flying around like swallows circling above our barnyard after sundown. Some of the words were:

There is no way out, there is no way back,
There is no other way but *through*.

We *had* to get through that cellar door and up into the house!

One thing we couldn't do, however. We couldn't just rush up to that big iron-reinforced door and say, "Open, sesame!" and expect it to open like the door to the robbers' den in "Ali Baba and the Forty Thieves."

The phone upstairs was still ringing. Or else it had stopped and was starting again. Or unless I had a ringing in the ears of my mind.

With nobody answering the phone, it meant there really was nobody up there, so it wouldn't do any good to start pounding on the door and yelling for somebody to come down and open it.

But Dragonfly must have thought it would, because he did start pounding on that door and yelling, "Help! Come down and let us in! *H–e–l–p!*"

We were like three rats in a trap. From the way my jaw felt, and the way that for some reason I couldn't see so well with my right eye, I knew that one of the bullies, or both, had very hard-knuckled fists and powerful muscles. If only Big Jim and Circus were here! Why did they have to go off to Tippecanoe County, anyway, when there was a law against boys under sixteen working for wages on a farm?

My father had been trying to teach me, "Don't be an if-only boy! Be a do-something-er!" But how, I ask you, can you *do* something when there isn't a thing you can do? If only this were a story on a radio program or a television drama, the hero could just ram his powerful shoulder against the door, and it would break open.

But the door we were on the wrong side of couldn't be broken through by three boys our size. If we tried it, we'd maybe get our shoulders broken instead.

I stepped back though, as if I was going to make a run for the door, and stumbled over Poetry, who right that minute was down on his knees, shining his light all around the sawdust-covered floor below the ledge where the key was supposed to have been.

I lost my balance, and down I went. As I put out my hands to stop myself from falling too hard, my right hand landed on something flat and long and the shape of a door key.

"I've found it!" I exclaimed in a husky whisper. "We're saved!"

I rolled over and onto my feet, dashed to the door, then let out a groan. What I had in my hand was only a thin flat chip of wood. I hadn't found the key, and we weren't saved!

Now there was *really* no way out and no way back. And there most certainly wasn't any way through!

"No way out, and no way back," I heard myself saying.

Poetry heard me, and he answered my worry with a surprisingly calm voice. "When there isn't any way of danger and no way through it or back, you just have to *live* your way through it. That's what my father says, which is maybe what that song means anyway."

My two good honest best friends beside me were doubled up, ready to help me in any way they could, as I answered Poetry, "If we *can* live!"

Behind us now came the barking voice of the biggest boy. "All right, you ornery little brats! We've got you now! You, there—the one with the box! Set it down and turn around and face the wall. All three of you! Hands over your heads!"

In the past we'd always had trouble with Dragonfly's stubbornness when he was ordered to do something he didn't want to do. In as saucy a voice now as I'd ever heard him use, he called back into that blinding flashlight, "I will not! It's our box! We found it, and we're going to keep it!"

The blinding light was moving slowly toward us. With my foot I felt a rock the size of a boy's doubled-up fist. If only I could make a quick stoop . . . grab up the rock . . .

But it was only another "if only." I started to

stoop and got stopped stock-still by a savage command.

"Don't be a fool, boy!"

The toughs kept walking toward us. The one with the flashlight was lighting the way for the other one, who right that second made a dive for Dragonfly to grab the box away from him.

But the littlest member of the Thompson, Gilbert, and Collins Frogs Legs Supply Company began to dodge this way and that and that way and this. For several exciting minutes he was like a mouse in a house with a woman with a broom after him, as he held onto the ribbon-wrapped box with both of his two good, honest best friends, diving and circling, ducking and whirling.

This way, that way, round and round, behind me, behind Poetry, Dragonfly kept on dodging, trying to keep from getting caught. And then, so fast I didn't even see it happen, Dragonfly sneak-passed the box to Poetry. And now *he* was the roly-poly mouse in a house with two women with two brooms after him.

Not being as wiry as Dragonfly and not able to dodge as fast, Poetry tried to use a little brute force instead. He was backed against the cave wall, with the light shining in his eyes, when the best half of his mind must have given him an idea. He lowered his head like Harm Groenwold's old red bull and charged straight for the stomach of the boy closest to him. The same boy whose stomach I had rammed into headfirst back near the lilacs was going to get whammed into again.

But this time the ruffian didn't double up with pain. Instead, he met Poetry's charge with his two *worst* friends, and gave Leslie Thompson a savage straight-down *wham-sock* on the back of his shoulders. And Poetry himself went down, not saved out of his trouble and not getting *through* it but slumped to his knees right in the middle of it.

On the way down, he squawked to me, "Let 'em have the box! We can get it back later!"

One of the rough, tough guys grabbed up the box from the cave floor, while the other held the light on us and barked fiercely, "Now, no more monkey business! Do as we say, and you won't get hurt. I have a knife pointed your way. See?"

I thought I did see something shining in his free hand as he moved to the cellar door, inserted a key in the lock, opened the door, and ordered us in.

And that's when I woke up to the fact that those boys had known not only the path that led to the cave but also the way through it, and where the basement door key was kept, and maybe a lot of other things only the Sugar Creek Gang was supposed to know.

We *had* to take orders, now that they had our box *and* a knife and might decide to use the knife on us if we didn't obey. But I tell you, it's one of the hardest things a boy ever has to do—to do something you're ordered to do when you don't want to.

Through the open door we went into Old Man Paddler's cellar. And that's when I heard the sound of rain on the clapboard roof of the old man's cabin. And the reason we could hear it was because the trapdoor at the top of the short stairway was open.

Like captured prisoners, with maybe a knife at our backs and with the brown box in the hands of our captors, we climbed those cellar steps to the old man's kitchen.

There we found for sure that they did have a switchblade. When I saw its gleaming steel, cold chills swept all over me, and I thought, *What if they had used it on us when we had had our fight at the branch bridge? Or what if we had been dumb enough to have tackled them down in the cave?*

We *had* to take orders now!

One of our captors lit the kerosene lamp on the kitchen table. The minute he did, I noticed that the window drapes were closed so that nobody outside could see in.

I also got a glimpse of the large map of the West Indies on the wall above the table, on which the old man had maybe a dozen different-colored pins in different places. One extralarge redheaded pin was right in the center of Palm Tree Island, where his twin brother, Kenneth, lived. Used to live, I mean.

Just seeing that redheaded pin, which the gang had seen so many times when we had visited the old man, was like a knife blade turning in my heart, because in my mind I was seeing another little brown box sitting on the top shelf of a Collins closet.

My eyes took in several other things as they made one quick sweep the minute the kerosene lamp was lit. There was a small camp stove on the kitchen worktable, and the sink was half filled with unwashed dishes—almost all the old man had for everyday use. The blanket on his double bed was wrinkled, as was also the usually neat bedspread, which meant somebody had probably been sleeping there.

Dragonfly was noticing other things and not just what he was seeing. All of a sudden he got a mussed-up expression on his face and let out a stormy sneeze.

He got a short, sharp order from one of our captors: "Stop that!"

But Dragonfly couldn't, because the kind of sneeze he gets when he smells something like what I myself was smelling right that minute is the kind nobody can stop.

The strange odor in the room was not the smell of cooking, or of camp stove gasoline, or of the kerosene lamp. It was different from the burning pine odor you get from a just-lit match.

My eyes took in a fast circle of everything, and I saw over on the old man's antique console table, one end of which was attached to the wall, a saucer half filled with ashes and cigarette butts. And that's when I realized that the strange odor in the room was the same kind I'd smelled earlier in the day—the odor of whirligig beetles stampeding in the shaded water near the mouth of the branch.

It was a very sickening odor—like too-ripe apples, or overripe papaws, or licorice mixed with moldy muskmelon. It was also like the smell of the poison leaves of the jimsonweeds that grow in barnyards around Sugar Creek territory.

My jaw went shut with temper when I saw the saucer the cigarette ashes were in. It was a very beautiful saucer that I knew belonged to a special set of chinaware the old man himself never used but kept behind glass doors in his wife's china closet.

That set of dishes was very rare, my mother had said once when she was visiting the old man with some of the other Sugar Creek mothers, taking measurements for the new drapes they were going to make for his windows. "Genuine bone china," Poetry's mother said, she being a member of the Quester's Club and having studied antiques. "Bone china," she explained, "is made of the very finest clays, mixed with bone ash."

Now why in the world would the words *bone ash* land with a splash in my mind at a time like that, unless somewhere back in a secret corner of it I was thinking about bone ashes in a box that had come in the mail from Palm Tree Island that very morning.

Knowing the old man himself never used any kind of ashtray, and that the only smoke you ever smelled in his cabin was the sweet woodsy smell of logs burning in his fireplace, and knowing how tenderhearted his thoughts always were for his wife, Sarah, who was buried under the big pine tree on Bumblebee Hill, and seeing and smelling the rotten papaw-smelling ashes in the bone china saucer—it all set my temper on edge.

Without knowing how mad I was, I all of a sudden exploded. "That saucer belongs to Sarah Paddler's antique bone china set! If she knew you used it for cigarette stubs and ashes, she'd turn over in her grave!"

One of the ruffians, I now noticed, had extralong curly hair reaching down to his shoulders. The other had short hair, which suddenly explained to my mind the reason they had motorcycled back to the lilac bushes. It was to try to find the *wig* Poetry had pulled off in our scuffle an hour earlier.

The one with the long curly hair was the one holding the knife and giving orders to the other one. He answered my word explosion by saying, "Listen, little boy! If you don't hold your tongue, you'll be lying face down in your *own* grave!"

In a fair fight the nine of us could have licked the six of them but not when there was a switchblade in the right worst friend of the older, savage-faced boy.

We had to let them do what they were doing right that minute, which was tying us, one at a time, into hardbacked chairs, with our hands behind us and our feet tied to the chair legs.

8

It took those rough, tough guys only a few minutes to tie up all three members of the Thompson, Gilbert, and Collins Frogs Legs Supply Company and to tape our mouths shut with adhesive tape.

And that's when the phone started ringing again. The boy with the switchblade knife, whose dark hair reached down to his shoulders, jumped as if he had been shot. He made a dive for the phone, not to answer it but to stop the shorter-haired boy from answering.

For a few minutes, there in the yellowish light of the kerosene lamp, it looked as though there might be a fight between our captors themselves, though the one with the knife looked savage enough to scare anybody into letting him be the boss. The other boy, who had just finished taping Dragonfly's mouth, was standing near the old man's woodbox, filled with the firewood that we, the Gang, had carried in for him. He stood now with squinting eyes and a worried look on his face. He spoke then, and his voice was kind of like the prodigal son's voice must have sounded—if anybody had heard it—and what he said was: "I'm tired of being a Son of Lucifer. I want to go home."

"Home!" the long-haired, bearded one sneered. "You mean back to the supermarket and the police station! You do remember the supermarket, don't you? And, of course, you remember *this!*" With that, he laid his right hand on the box, still tied with the knotted red ribbon.

The phone rang. It must have rung seven or eight times before it stopped. Then it started again, and this time I counted the rings— exactly seven before it stopped.

That's when I heard a new sound beside me. It was Dragonfly whimpering and straining in his chair as if he was fighting for every breath he was taking through his nose.

The next thing I knew, the junior member of the Thompson, Gilbert, and Collins Frogs Legs Supply Company had tilted his chair sideways, and over he went *thump-thump-ker-thump* onto the kitchen floor. At the same time there was a sound *outside* the cabin like the rumble of thunder, along with another sound like a scraping or scratching and a thump-thump-thumping on the metal roof of the old man's upstairs back porch.

And now, still another sound—a little like thunder but a little more like a boy playing the drums. And *then* a loud voice from maybe as far away as the old man's woodshed said, "All right in there! You're surrounded! Come on out with your hands up!"

Even though the startling voice outside sounded as if it was coming through a bullhorn being used by the sheriff or the police, and maybe it meant we were going to be rescued, still, for some reason, it didn't make me feel happy. I'd been sort of hoping we could figure out our own way to free ourselves and get back the stolen box.

And then things began to happen fast there in the cabin. While Dragonfly was struggling around on the floor, still tied to his turned-over chair, while the rain was dinning on the roof, while the thundery voice outside was bellowing like a monster bullfrog—right in the mixed-up middle of all that excitement, I saw a wild look come into the eyes of the fierce-faced bearded boy with the knife. He quickly grabbed up the flashlight, which was on the table beside the box, scooped up the box itself, rushed to the open trapdoor, and down he went like a scared bullfrog with a boy carrying a gunnysack after him.

I heard the big wooden door downstairs squeak on its hinges and then footsteps running back into the cave, *crunch-crunch-crunchety-crunch-crunch-crunch,* getting farther and farther away.

In my mind's eye I saw a picture in one of our school readers of Peter Rabbit running for his life to get away from Mr. McGregor, who was chasing him with a rake.

But that was only for a fleeting second. What my imagination began fast to imagine was that long-bearded, long-haired fugitive swerving this way and that, hurrying, hurrying, hurrying toward the mouth of the cave. I saw him coming out just above the base of the sycamore tree, leaping down, racing in the path along the creek to the boat, and on and on and on and still on to the lilacs, then swinging onto the motorcycle and roaring away, taking the little brown box with him and hurrying with it to Mary Jane Moragrifa somewhere for the reward.

Inside the cabin, the beardless, short-haired Son of Lucifer stood as if he didn't know what on earth to do. He was like a rambler rose somebody had torn the trellis away from, and it didn't have anything to cling to.

Now, also, the phone, which was only a few feet from where I was still tied to my chair, began ringing again. And this time the short-haired boy picked it up and listened a few seconds. As plain as day, I heard a husky voice saying, "Raid! There's going to be a raid. Hide everything!"

The phone went *click* on the other end. The blue-eyed, beardless boy looked wildly around the room, started toward the trapdoor, stopped, then jumped as the thundery bull-horn outside called again. "We're giving you to the count of ten. One–two–three–four–"

At the count of five, our captor swung toward Sarah Paddler's walnut bureau-cabinet, took a key out of his jeans pocket, and with hurrying, trembling hands fitted it into the lock of one of the bureau's two doors. While he had his back to us and was turning the key, I noticed his boylike face in the mirror, and I wondered what he was *really* afraid of.

The minute the cabinet door was open, I saw on the lower shelf a package the size and shape of the one the bearded boy had just dived down the cellar steps with.

Another brown box!

That younger boy took another worried look all around and said to us, "I hate to leave you tied up, but the police'll get you loose." With that, he grabbed up Poetry's flashlight, and away he went down the cellar stairs, taking the second box with him.

Dragonfly, on the floor beside the telephone, was squirming and grunting, and his face was getting a mussed-up expression as if he was having an even harder time breathing. That really scared me. I knew that whenever he was especially allergic to anything he was near, his nose would swell shut, and he would have to breathe through his mouth. But how could he breathe through his mouth when it was taped shut? *How could he breathe at all?*

I began to struggle fiercely with the ropes around my wrists and tried to yell to whoever was outside to come on in. It was like being in a dream in which you are in some terrible danger and are trying to call for help and you can't say a word. But you try and try and try and try. And it was maybe almost the most terrible feeling I had had in my whole life.

Until death do us part, I thought desperately. If only I could yell to whoever was outside to come on in.

I looked at Poetry in his chair beside me,

and he was fighting as hard as I was to get his hands untied.

The count of ten had already been reached, and in another second something would happen. Something would *have* to happen.

And something *did* happen. There was the sound now of hurrying steps on the porch and a banging on the door—banging and banging and banging—and then, from upstairs, came the sound of a window opening, as if somebody up there was going out or maybe coming in.

And now that somebody was already in! I could see him at the head of the stairs.

It was another boy, one without a beard.

From the top of the stairway there came down now, two steps at a time, a curly-haired athletic-looking boy with a tape recorder in one hand, and it was Circus Browne, the acrobat of our gang!

What on earth! And *double* what on earth! Circus's eyes took in a quick circle of directions, saw us all tied up in our chairs, saw Dragonfly red-faced and struggling for breath. He flew into action and in a flash had Dragonfly's mouth free. Then he rushed to the door, unbolted it, and threw it wide open, letting in another person—not the sheriff, or the police deputy, or another law-enforcement officer but good old powerful-muscled, fuzzy-mustached, keen-thinking, clean-living Big Jim, our leader!

Big Jim took one sweeping look around the cabin and at us and asked, "What on earth is going on here?"

Dragonfly, with his voice free and able to breathe, started to explain. "We g–g–got k–k–kidnapped! They were going to hold us for r–r–ransom!" That shows what he had been thinking about while we were tied up.

Poetry's mouth was untaped next, then mine, and our hands and feet were untied, and we all started talking at once.

Circus got in a few words, explaining why he and Big Jim were there. "We found out you were going to stay all night in Poetry's guesthouse, so we made a tape to scare you a little, just for fun. Then when you weren't there and there wasn't any light, we wondered if maybe you might have decided to stay here instead. We knew you had, or we *thought* you had, when we saw light filtering through the window drapes, and that's how come—*listen!*"

Circus pressed a switch on the tape recorder, and there was the beginning of what sounded like a snare drum rolling. Then there came thundering out: *"All right, in there! You're surrounded! Come out with your hands up!"*

Circus turned off the recorder's playback switch. It would have been a good joke if it had been, but it wasn't.

And right that minute there was another and different sound—not outside or upstairs but down in the cellar. Not way back in the cave somewhere, either, but in the room next to the basement, close to where the old man kept the door key.

In the lamplight we looked into all our startled faces, wondering what on earth and why, and who was down there, and had they maybe been down there all the time, listening.

And now there was the sound of footsteps rushing toward the cellar steps. In another minute we would know what on earth and why and who!

I guessed why, when from back deep in the cave, we heard now an actual bullhorn and a deep, thundery voice calling and echoing through the cavern and saying, "Listen, Darrel! This is your father! Give yourself up! Your mother's crying her heart out!"

My mind grabbed a memory then, and it was what the beardless boy had said quite a while ago to the long-haired one, *"I'm tired of being a Son of Lucifer! I want to go home!"*

In my mind's eye was another memory also, and it was of a reddish brown mustached father sitting at a kitchen table with an open Bible and saying across to his wife, "Nobody went after the prodigal son. He had to get fed up with the disgusting life he was living."

The memory got interrupted by fast action, faster than anybody could imagine. I heard it before I saw it, and then I saw it. Up those cellar steps came the long-haired bearded boy, carrying a box wrapped round and round with red ribbon. And in the other hand, ready to stab anybody who tried to stop him, was a gleaming switchblade knife.

There was other action in the room then. It was Big Jim, rushing to the door, making sure it was bolted. And there he stood, his back to the door, his two best friends at his side, his eyes on the knife, his body tense. I knew there was going to be a fierce fight of some kind. It would not be a fistfight, though, but the kind of battle two boys have when one of them has a weapon and that weapon is a knife.

But Big Jim wasn't the only member of the Sugar Creek Gang who was on the side of the law. There were four other boys, each one with two good, honest best friends and with a mind apiece to help him think.

I remembered one other thing my father had said that day across the table: *The way of the transgressor is hard.* And right that minute it seemed it was the whole gang's business to help make that boy's life a little harder for him.

I picked up the chair I had been tied to a little while before.

At the same time Dragonfly grabbed a stick of wood out of the woodbox. He raced over to stand beside Big Jim, and, with a savage voice, quoted a line from a poem we had had in school the year before, saying,

"'Shoot, if you must, this old gray head, but spare your country's flag,' she said!"

It was ridiculous to say a thing like that at a time like that. Nobody had a gun with which to shoot, and Dragonfly didn't have an old gray head!

The bearded one with the knife doubled

himself into a crouch and started moving toward the door Big Jim still had his back to, while the rest of us stayed behind him, ready to do anything we could. One thing was for sure: we were *not* going to let him get out that door with our box!

Behind me there was a stealthy movement, and I caught a glimpse of it without turning my head. There on the floor on his hands and knees was Leslie Poetry Thompson. I knew in a flash what he was doing and what he wanted one of the rest of the gang to do.

I moved with my chair toward the woodbox and sprang around in front of the bully with the knife. Holding the chair legs ahead of me like a lion tamer in a circus, I started toward him, yelling, "Back! Back! Get back!"

I was in a half crouch myself now, imagining myself facing a fierce-fanged Bengal tiger. Then I gave a shove with the chair and a run at the same time, and that's also when the Son of Lucifer with the knife and the box stumbled backward over Poetry's body. Down he went, striking his head on a corner of Sarah Paddler's antique walnut bureau.

Like a streak of powerful-muscled fury, Big Jim was across the room, and the battle for the knife was on.

Almost on, that is. Big Jim got stopped by the same sprawled roly-poly boy the bearded one had gotten stopped by, and down *he* went.

Up rolled the Bengal tiger. He took a wild-eyed look at us and gave a worried listen to the bullhorn, which right that second came bellowing up from the cellar, "We're coming up!" He dashed for the stairway down which Circus had come only a little while before.

No sooner had the bearded one gone clumping up the stairs, than there was a scramble of footsteps coming up from the cellar. Right away the cabin was full of boys and men. The boys were us, and the men were our favorite sheriff, Jim Colbert, and two of his deputies, all three of them wearing shining badges. And with them was the short-haired, beardless boy and a worried-faced neatly mustached man who looked like him and might have been his father.

We were all there except Circus. And then I heard him yelling from outside the cabin, "Come on out, everybody! Help! *Help!*"

9

In less time than it would take me to write it for you even in shorthand—if I could write it that way, which I can't—Sheriff Jim Colbert and his two deputies and all the rest of the gang, as well as the beardless boy and his maybe father were outdoors in the rain helping Circus capture a runaway tiger.

There were flashlights with lights crossing and crisscrossing all around, shining on the railing of the upstairs porch, the open window up there, and the rainwater gushing from the downspout into a little cement spillway and through it to the outer edge of the patio.

Things were happening so fast that it was hard to see what was going on. It was like being in a big outdoor room, with giant-sized pictures all over all the walls and all the pictures having fast-moving people in them.

Then I saw the long-haired Son of Lucifer. He was way over on the other side of the upstairs porch where the ladder was, swinging his legs over the balustrade. In a minute, I thought, he would be down that ladder. He would then race across the old man's patio, dive down the steep hill there, and get away. He could lose himself in the woods and maybe not get captured at all.

I had almost forgotten Darrel Inwood, but that's when he flew into action. Like a quail exploding out of its hiding place in a fencerow when a dog comes trotting through the shrubbery, he shot out of our circle toward that ladder, yelling to all of us behind him, "Help, everybody!"

He got to the bottom of the ladder just as the bearded boy's feet found the top rung and just as Jim Colbert got there. It was like watching a circus act to see what happened next. Jim Colbert and Darrel Inwood swung the top of that ladder out away from the porch gutter, and there, in the light of all the flashlights, was a boy with a beard on the top of a straight-up ladder five feet out from the porch. He was swaying in the air, but not with the greatest of ease. He was holding on for dear life with the two worst best friends a boy ever had.

There was no way up, and no way down, and no other way but nowhere.

But the Son of Lucifer at the top of the ladder, with no way up and no way down, started to climb. Then, like a flying squirrel taking off from a high tree, he swung his body out and leaped off—landing in the arms of two deputies. In less than sixteen seconds he was handcuffed and a prisoner of the law.

They handcuffed Darrel Inwood also, because both boys had been fugitives from the law for quite a while.

Because it was still raining, it seemed like a good idea to go back into the cabin, which we did, getting in just as the telephone began ringing again. Jim Colbert picked up the phone, which happened to be not more than a foot from my outstretched hand at the time, and, as before, there was a voice saying loud enough for me to hear, "Hide everything."

The phone went *click*.

Like a sphinx moth darting from a petunia to a tiger lily in Mom's flower garden, the sheriff dialed a number from memory, one he had maybe called again and again in his business of enforcing the law.

The minute somebody answered on the other end of the line, he barked an order, saying, "Raid the Cliff Cottage. Surround it first so nobody can get across the bridge into the woods."

To us he explained, "There's a drug ring in the neighborhood, headed by a woman who calls herself Oliver Twist. She'd been using some motorcycle gangs to help deliver. Some of the boys who work for her are young runaways. She supplied them with wigs."

Poetry and I interrupted our listening long enough to look each other in the eye and nod our heads.

My mind darted back to Jim Colbert's explanation in time to hear him saying, "She moved into Cliff Cottage at the Bay Tree Inn about noon today. It would have made a perfect headquarters for her, with the footbridge, the dense woods, the island, the cave, and with Seneth Paddler in California. I guess she didn't reckon on you boys—or else didn't figure you'd be any problem, with half of you out of the neighborhood. There were only three of you, I believe—"

Dragonfly cut in to say, "There were *nine* of us!" He stopped as soon as he had started and grinned at Poetry and me.

Well, there were a lot of other things the Sugar Creek Gang wanted to know about what was going on and why. First of all, what was in the box on the table below Old Man Paddler's prayer map?

The sheriff sniffed the air in the room. Then he spotted Sarah Paddler's bone china saucer with the cigarette butts in it. Some of the stubs were larger than others, looking as if they had been hand rolled. And then he took a close-up smell.

"Roaches!"

I was surprised at that, because as many times as I had been in the old man's always clean cabin, I'd never seen any cockroaches. And there weren't any, dead or alive, in the saucer.

Jim Colbert must have heard my gasp, because he said with a grin, "A *roach* is a *reefer,* and a *reefer* is a marijuana cigarette."

"And here," one of the deputies said, "is another of Oliver's aliases." He lifted the little brown box, still tied with its tangle of red ribbon, moved with it to the lamp, and read aloud: "For liberal reward, return to Mary Jane Moragrifa."

With the switchblade knife, the deputy cut the ribbon and in a few seconds had the box open.

Beside me, Dragonfly, who was also trying to see what was inside, sneezed and dropped back out of the circle.

"Perfect manicure," the deputy said. "Oliver's finest brand."

Well, that was the reason the box had been so important to the Sons of Lucifer. It was filled with hundreds of dollars' worth of Mary Jane, which, the sheriff told us, was pure marijuana.

Behind us Dragonfly let out another sneeze and exclaimed, "I smell whirligig beetles!" He didn't, of course, but his nose was saying *no* to the sickeningly sweet odor of what Jim Colbert told us, a few minutes later, was ruining the bodies and especially the minds of so many young people and causing pastors, teachers, doctors, and parents so much worry.

The minute the sheriff mentioned "parents," I was startled by the beardless Son of Lucifer interrupting him to say, "If you boys' parents don't know where you are, you'd better phone 'em and let 'em know, so they won't worry."

I was *not* surprised right then to remember one of the most interesting stories in the Bible. It was about a boy who had run away from home. After a long time, when he was feeding pigs for a job and hungry enough to eat hog food, he came to himself right in the pigpen and started running back to his father's house.

I looked quick at Darrel Inwood. He was standing beside his father, who, when his son said that, swallowed a lump in his throat and tightened his arm around his boy's shoulders.

In less than three minutes, maybe, Big Jim, Poetry, Circus, and Dragonfly had telephoned their parents. Then it was my turn.

When my father answered and asked, "Where on earth have you boys been? What have you been doing? We've phoned all over for you!" I answered, "We've been helping the sheriff capture a couple of the Devil's angels. We're at Old Man Paddler's cabin now, but we'll be home as soon as we can."

For some reason, my Farm Bureau speaker father wasn't satisfied—not until Sheriff Colbert himself took the phone and explained.

Of course, we didn't get to spend the night at Poetry's as we had planned. All of us, including Darrel Inwood and the surly-faced other boy, went back down through the cave and to the branch bridge. From there one of the deputies drove the members of the gang to our different homes, while Jim Colbert drove his own car as fast as he could to the Bay Tree Inn to see what was going on there. And quite a lot was, I found out later.

The news came in on the deputy's car radio just as we were getting in. I missed part of it because all of a sudden there was a startling sound only a few feet behind me. It was like a young calf learning to bawl and getting choked.

And do you know what? Dragonfly had

accidentally stepped on a gunnysack that had seven bullfrogs in it, and one of the frogs in bullfrogs' language had croaked, "*Ou–ou–ou–ouch!*"

My mind leaped back to the car radio in time to hear, "Oliver was in the middle of the footbridge with no way across and no way back, so she tried to climb over the railing and fell. The ambulance has taken her to the hospital."

We drove home with $3.50 worth of frogs on the floor of the car at our feet.

At the Collins house next noon, our family talked it all over, after having talked about it part of the night before and most of the morning. There certainly was a lot of new news for the gang, for the parents of the neighborhood, and also for the reporters who came from all over to see what was going on.

We found out there would have to be a court hearing for the Sons of Lucifer we had captured in Old Man Paddler's cabin and also for Oliver Twist, just as soon as the doctor said she was able to leave the hospital.

The island, we learned, had been the secret hiding place for the marijuana that Oliver and her gang had been selling, and they had been using *our boat* to ride over in.

And from the deputy who drove us home, we'd learned a lot of things every boy ought to know about how hard the way of the transgressor is.

At lunch I was maybe bragging a little to my

parents as I told about my battle with the savage Bengal tiger and as I explained, *"Mary Jane* is slanguage for marijuana, and *Moragrifa is* another name for it. *Manicure* is high-grade marijuana which has been cleaned and has no stems or seeds."

In my mind, as I talked to my parents—who maybe didn't know much about what was going on in the country—I was the deputy. I repeated what he had told us in the car: "Anyone who smokes marijuana runs the risk of ruining his health and even his mind. Many people go from marijuana to stronger drugs and get themselves handcuffed to the Devil."

I got stopped in my speech by my mother saying to my father, "It seems that sometimes a father *does* go after his prodigal son—like Darrel's father did."

"I'm afraid Darrel Inwood's father was a prodigal *father,*" my dad answered. "He was a successful businessman but a complete failure as a father. And his mother loved her clubs and parties more than she loved her own boy. That's *partly* why he ran away. He thought the gang he was running around with loved him. But they only wanted to get him hooked and make him a pusher."

Mom had a faraway look in her eyes as she said across her plate of hash brown potatoes, ham, and applesauce to her husband, who was eating again, "Love is kind, but it sometimes has to be very firm. Love means discipline, but love is selfless. And love takes time."

Then my father turned toward me and said from under his reddish brown mustache, "You need a haircut, Son, before Sunday. I don't want the neighborhood thinking our son is a monster or a caveman."

That took my mind back to our own cave and to all the excitement we had had there last night—and to the battle for the box among the lilacs. It wasn't any time to try to be funny, but I answered my father, "Until my hair gets long enough, I could maybe wear a wig."

The phone rang then, and Dad went to answer it. When he came back into the kitchen, he had a very serious look on his face. "It was Seneth Paddler. He's at the airport. He sounded pretty shaken up over the news about his brother. He is going to need all the love we can give him for the next few days and weeks."

That brought my thoughts back to the box on the top shelf of our upstairs closet—the ashes of Old Man Paddler's twin brother, Kenneth, who had asked that he be buried in the cemetery on the slope of Strawberry Hill.

After lunch, while my father was driving to the airport to get Old Man Paddler, and while my mother was in the living room typing the last chapter to the book *The Christian After Death,* and while I was proving that love is a many-splendored thing by washing the dishes, and Charlotte Ann was helping by getting in the way, it seemed I wanted to go upstairs for a while just to be alone with my thoughts.

I stopped at the living room door before

heading for the stairs and said toward Mom's flying typewriter keys, "I have the dishes washed and rinsed and in the drainer, letting nature dry them. I think I need a *thought* break."

Mom looked up with a faraway expression and also tears, I thought, in her eyes. She nodded. "I've been up several times today myself."

For some reason after I reached the top of the steps, I slowed down and was walking on tiptoe when I went through the north room door. The little brown box, I noticed, had been moved from the closet shelf and was sitting on the dresser in front of the wide mirror. From the angle I was looking at it, its reflection in the mirror was as clear as the box itself. For a second, it seemed I was looking at *twin* boxes, one in the room and the other in another room on the other side of a window. Even though it was a sad thought, at the same time it made me glad to be alive in a real body with a real mind and to think I probably had a long life ahead of me.

From the woods across the gravel road there was the happy sound of different kinds of birds singing. I could see Strawberry Hill and the tall old pine tree that grew there. From its top branches a flock of blackbirds took off as though they were in a hurry to go somewhere in their blackbird world. It was too early in the season for blackbirds to gather themselves into flocks for their flight to a warmer part of the United States to spend the winter. They always waited until September to do that.

I watched them—maybe fifty or more—flying helter-skelter toward the trees in the bayou. Then I turned back to take another look at the two brown boxes on the dresser.

A happy thought came into my mind then, though it was a little sad too. It was: *Kenneth Paddler doesn't live in this world anymore. His spirit has gone to a very special place—not just for the winter, but forever.*

My mind came all the way back to the Collins family world when I heard Charlotte Ann starting to come up the steps. I quickly hurried to the head of the stairs and called down to her, "Love is a two-way stairway! You come on up, and I'll come on down, and we'll meet each other halfway."

Halfway down, I swooped my chubby little mischievous-minded sister up into my brawny arms, which at the time felt strong as iron bands like the Village Blacksmith's, and carried her giggling and kicking all the way down to the bottom step, through the kitchen, and outdoors.

The minute the screen door slammed behind us, old Mixy, our black-and-white cat, looked up from her afternoon catnap near the grape arbor and came stretching and yawning toward us as if she was the most contented and best-loved cat in the world with all her nine lives still ahead of her.

Hearing a sound from the direction of the twin hickory nut trees, I looked up the road and saw a pickup driving through the gate that leads toward Strawberry Hill. The decal on the side of the truck said "The Sugar Creek Nursery."

In the back of the truck was what looked like a four-foot-tall evergreen, just the right size for a Christmas tree, standing as straight as if it were growing along the creek or the bayou.

I didn't get to find out what the very pretty, extragreen evergreen was for until two days later at Kenneth Paddler's funeral.

It seemed nearly everybody in Sugar Creek territory was on Strawberry Hill that afternoon. There were cars and cars and more cars parked everywhere. Some of them were in the woods at the bottom of the hill. One was only a few feet from the Little Jim Tree, where, in one of the gang's most exciting experiences, Little Jim had killed a fierce old mother bear.

I hadn't realized there were so many older people—some of them *extra*old—living in our part of the county. They were people who used to know Kenneth Paddler when he was a boy, when he used to live here and go to school, and a few had hunted and fished with him and his twin brother.

All the gang were there, even Little Jim, whose uncle had driven him all the way back from Wisconsin.

During the service, our pastor and Old Man Paddler and all of us boys stood in the shade of the big pine tree only a few feet from Sarah Paddler's tombstone. We were also close to where the Sugar Creek Nursery had planted the neat little spruce tree that was going to be Kenneth Paddler's memorial—a live evergreen instead of a monument of granite or marble.

First, there was the sweetest organ music anybody ever heard. I didn't know where it was coming from until I saw Little Jim's mother on the other side of the spruce tree, sitting at a small battery-powered organ, and the hymn she was playing was "Beyond the Sunset."

A male quartet from our church sang three verses of the song "We'll Say Good Night Here, but Good Morning Up There." Then our minister read from the Bible.

From where I was, I could see all the people standing on the hillside, stretching all the way to the top and around in a wide semicircle, looking and listening, and some of them wiping tears from their eyes.

For a few seconds my thoughts took off on a flying trip into the past, like milkweed seeds floating away on their flossy parachutes. Strawberry Hill was maybe one of the most important places in the whole territory. Everybody else in the neighborhood called it by that name, but the Sugar Creek Gang called it Bumblebee Hill because it was on this hillside that we had been forced into a rough-and-tumble battle with a tough town gang and had stumbled and rolled onto a bumblebees' nest. In only a few seconds the fight was over.

And now there was something going on at the little tree beside and behind which the gang was standing, not more than a few feet from the organ and Old Man Paddler himself. It was Willard Kincaid, the undertaker, opening the little brown box.

As soon as the wrapping was off, he lifted out a small metal container about the size of a two-pound coffee can. Then they had what is called the "interment." Willard Kincaid began to carefully pour out all the silver gray ashes into the little circular well they had left around the base of the tree.

Then Mr. Kincaid took a shovel and carefully covered all the ashes with yellowish brown soil. After that, standing with the rest of us with bowed heads, he waited until our minister said in a voice loud enough for all to hear, "Ashes to ashes, dust to dust."

All of a sudden Old Man Paddler stepped away from the tree, lifted his trembling old right hand—the best right hand any man ever had, I thought—and signaled that he wanted to say something.

The best I can remember, this is part of what he said: "For the Christian, after death means, first of all, *absent from the body . . . at home with the Lord.*' One thing is good to remember —that a person is not saved by *being* good or by *doing* good. The door to heaven is not opened to us by any good thing we can do or by anything religious any person can do *to us*. Salvation is by grace through faith in the Lord Jesus Christ.

"I am sure that if my brother, Kenneth, was able to tell me what he wanted said at his funeral, it would be: 'Tell everyone that I died trusting in Christ as my very own personal Savior.'"

The old man stopped, took a deep breath, and looked toward the crest of the hill. His snow-white hair and beard shining in the afternoon sun made me think of a picture in our family's Bible story book showing Moses standing on a mountain with the Ten Commandments in his hands.

Others must have been thinking the same thing at the same time, because Little Jim, standing beside me, whispered, "Moses. He looks like Moses!"

Everything was so quiet for a minute, with the maybe three hundred people standing and waiting and thinking, that I was actually holding my breath.

Nature, though, didn't seem to realize what was going on. All of a sudden, from the fencerow over at the edge of the cemetery, a meadowlark let out a very fast, juicy-noted song that sounded like *"Spring of the year!"* A friendly little breeze came tumbling in from the woods, stirring up a half dozen or more dry leaves and pushing them toward the little mound of yellow brown soil, where they stopped near the tree trunk as though maybe they thought the ashes ought to be covered a little deeper.

I got one of the nicest surprises of my life right then. There came skimming across the open space between us and the fencerow a pair of yellow-rumped warblers. One of them lit in the brand-new evergreen and the other in a patch of last year's dead grass. Their movements were very fast, and the neat little bird noises they were making sounded as if they thought this would be a good place for their next year's nest. They quickly took off again in the direction of the Little Jim Tree when the organ started playing again.

The quartet sang another song. And in only a little while, after our pastor prayed a short prayer, the funeral was over.

Slowly and with everybody talking quietly, all the people began to leave. Some came down to where Old Man Paddler was, to shake his hand. Some of the mothers kissed him on his white-whiskered cheek. One of the women, I noticed, was my own wonderful, tenderhearted mother, who had to look away quickly to hide the tears she had been holding back as long as she could.

While the crowd was breaking up—some going one way and some another, fanning out all over the hill and into the woods—the gang decided that, before going to our different homes, we would go down to the spring for a drink of cold water.

At the top of the incline near the leaning linden tree, I stopped, noticing another neat little spruce tree growing beside the pasture rosebush. As many hundred times as I had passed that friendly little tree, it had never seemed important. But now, for some reason, it was maybe one of the prettiest evergreens there ever was.

I didn't realize Little Jim had stopped, too, until from beside me he said in a half whisper, "When Old Man Paddler dies, why don't they dig up this little tree and plant it right beside the other one?"

After saying that, the maybe best boy Christian in the whole territory took off on the run down the incline to the spring where the rest of the gang already was.

Before following him, I stood for a few seconds more, watching six or seven honeybees work the pink, five-petal rose blossoms, gathering nectar to carry back through the woods and across the Collins family yard to store it away in the hives in my father's apiary.

A very glad feeling came into my mind then. I turned and started on the run down to the spring.

As soon as I had had my drink, I stooped, picked up a handful of small flat stones, raced to the creek bank, and began skipping them across Sugar Creek's sober, foam-freckled face.

In a few jiffies, most of the rest of the gang was doing the same thing.

With rocks landing *skippety-skip-skip-skip*, with arms and hands like that many windmill sails flying, Dragonfly said, "It sure feels fine to be all together again—all eighteen of us."

Poetry, hearing him, answered, "We'll have to catch at least eighteen frogs a night just to make fifty cents apiece."

As if to answer Poetry's try at being funny, all of a sudden from behind us there came the sound of a monster bullfrog going *"G-g-g-r-r-rump!"*

I turned around in a hurry, knowing that bullfrogs don't bellow in the daylight. And there, not more than fifteen feet from the place where the spring water comes gurgling out of its metal pipe, was Circus, squatting like a hundred-pound tailless amphibian and grinning like a monkey. He exploded again, three or four times in succession, with croaks that sounded even more like a bullfrog than a bullfrog does.

Dragonfly was right. It certainly did feel fine to be all together again.

We would have to change the name of the Thompson, Gilbert, and Collins Frogs Legs Supply Company to a shorter name, I thought. We could maybe just call it the Sugar Creek Frogs Legs Supply. Even though the name "Collins" wouldn't be in it, at least it wouldn't have to be last, as it had been.

One thing was for sure—the Sugar Creek Gang was going to be together for better or for worse, for richer or poorer—especially *poorer*—until death do us part.

Moody Press, a ministry of the Moody Bible Institute,
is designed for education, evangelization, and edification.
If we may assist you in knowing more about Christ
and the Christian life, please write us without obligation:
Moody Press, c/o MLM, Chicago, Illinois 60610.